"*Trust,* touched my mind. *Trust that you are loved.*

Loved, I thought. Why did that matter now? All sacrifices were loved. That's why they're sacrificed.

I looked away from Ivan just as Dracula ran his pike through my chest....

— VAMPIRE CURSED

VAMPIRE CURSED

NORTHERN CREATURES BOOK TWO

KRIS AUSTEN RADCLIFFE

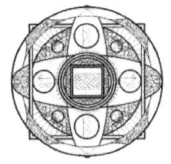

THE WORLDS OF
KRIS AUSTEN RADCLIFFE

Smart Urban Fantasy:

Northern Creatures

Monster Born

Vampire Cursed

Elf Raised

Wolf Hunted

Fae Touched

Death Kissed

God Forsaken

Magic Scorned

Witch Burned (*coming soon*)

Genre-bending Science Fiction about
love, family, and dragons:

WORLD ON FIRE

Series one

Fate Fire Shifter Dragon

Games of Fate

Flux of Skin

Fifth of Blood

Bonds Broken & Silent

All But Human

Men and Beasts

The Burning World

Dragon's Fate and Other Stories

Series Two

Witch of the Midnight Blade

Witch of the Midnight Blade Part One

Witch of the Midnight Blade Part Two

Witch of the Midnight Blade Part Three

Witch of the Midnight Blade: The Complete Series

Series Three

World on Fire

Call of the Dragonslayer (*coming soon*)

Hot Contemporary Romance:

The Quidell Brothers

Thomas's Muse

Daniel's Fire

Robert's Soul

Thomas's Need

Quidell Brothers Box Set

Includes:

Thomas's Muse

Daniel's Fire

Roberts's Soul

VAMPIRE CURSED

NORTHERN CREATURES
Book Two

By
Kris Austen Radcliffe

Six Talon Sign Fantasy & Futuristic Romance
Minneapolis

www.krisaustenradcliffe.com

First print edition, November 2017
Version: 10.19.2022

ISBN: 978-1-939730-54-1

VAMPIRE CURSED

CHAPTER 1

She told me her name was Ellie Jones and that I wouldn't remember her in the morning. She smiled a small, sad smile when she said it, one of those knowing smiles that made me believe she had lost hope. Ellie Jones believed that no matter what happened, come morning, she would be an afterthought.

Magic wafted around her like thin wisps of blue, purple, and green smoke. Not strong, obviously organized magic, but where she walked, subtle sheets of Aurora Borealis energy trailed.

The same magic that moved her to this place. Magic hurt her friend and it hurt her. It picked her up and it thrashed her against the rocks of my shore.

The magic meant she spoke the truth. Only magic could enchant and conceal—and wipe memories. Only magic could weigh on some-one's shoulders the way it weighed on hers.

"I will remember you," I said. There were ways around enchantments.

I came to this side of my lake—through the woods of the peninsula to the span of water out of view of my home—looking for my lost dog.

I found him, and he'd found Ellie.

Marcus Aurelius, in his grand hound way, found her alone and in pain. He stayed at her side and he led her down to the water.

The lake lapped the shore under the morning sun, and crisp early-autumn air cleansed away most of my vampiric problems from the night before, but it did little for Ellie.

She tugged on her hoodie, then pushed her enticing, shimmery, auburn-red hair behind her ear and looked down at the pebbles under her feet. Marcus Aurelius barked. And I think I fell in love.

Such a stupid thought. Such an utterly immature reaction to an unknown woman. I should damned well know better.

"You won't," she said. "The enchantments are layered."

No one deserved to drown under concealment enchantments or to vanish into the mist of spells woven expressly to obscure. No one.

She teetered on the slick pebbles and I stuck my hands into my pockets to keep from offering an uninvited touch.

Yet she moved as if her leg carried the majority of her pain—as if the magic that moved her here had settled in her thigh.

No more. I would not allow it to make her vanish—or be hurt—yet again.

I wanted to pick her up and carry her to the flat and stable trail, and to get her the help she needed for her wounds. To help and to make sure she no longer suffered.

But that would be presumptuous.

She dug in her hoodie's front pocket. "I..." Her expression opened, then closed, then opened again, as if she could not decide if trusting me was wise.

I almost reached for her again, but exercise and the sun had yet to fully warm my cold body. The last thing I wanted was to frighten her more with my corpse-like touch.

She peered at the tattoo on the side of my head. "I have an ash tree in my garden," she said in an offhand way.

From the lower muscles of my neck to the protection spells tattooed along the shaved scalp above my ears, the World Ash Yggdrasil climbed my scars and spread her branches. The elves had gifted me the magicks I wear—the protections, the tracer spells along the inside of my forearms, Yggdrasil's symbolism of unity and life.

And Ellie Jones spoke of an ash tree in her garden.

We did have a connection. But again, I would not be presumptuous.

"My friend," she said. "The one I lost. She took this photo." Ellie pulled from the pocket of her hoodie a daguerreotype photograph sheathed in a soft, sigil-marked sleeve.

She handed me the plate. "Have you ever met a seer?" she asked.

Seers carried witch blood, yet the subtle aurora of magic encircling the plate did not indicate *witch*. None of Ellie's magic twitched. Nothing snatched. Ellie Jones was not corrupted.

"Yes," I said as I took the plate. I'd met many seers in my two hundred years, but none of them had carried the beauty or sadness of the woman before me.

She tapped the sleeve. "Do you know what a daguerreotype is?"

Daguerreotype plates were the most-used photography method when I fought for the Union during the Civil War. "I haven't seen one in ages."

"Some seers use cards. Some crystals. I take and read photos."

I peered at the sigil on the sleeve. "That's complicated, isn't it?" Most seers used instant-read methods—tossed bones, tea leaves, cards and crystals, like Ellie said.

"The photos allow me to see magic," she whispered.

I'd never before met anyone who also saw magic. My ability was most likely an accident manifesting from my patchwork nature and my father's genius—if unholy—rewiring of my re-animated body. Ellie needed tools, but still, we walked this common ground.

And I would not remember her in the morning.

I had to remember her. I had to.

"The photo in that sleeve needs rinsing. I couldn't at my cottage. My pump isn't working," she said.

She needed my help. "Do you want me to look?" I could do this for her.

Her eyes widened. "If you would."

"I should take it out of the sleeve and wash it in the lake?"

She nodded *yes*.

I squatted next to the water and pulled the plate from the sheath. Like all daguerreotypes, its silver coating shimmered in the sunlight. Ellie had already developed it, and fixed the image, and now it needed a good rinse to make it visible.

I dipped the plate into the water once, then twice, but I still could not quite make out the image. I dipped it again.

I had no idea what I was looking at other than a clear image of a magical distortion wave moving through a room in what must be Ellie's home.

In the photo, her body radiated agony. The wave must have also hurt her friend, who was behind the camera and whom I did not see.

Behind Ellie, the wave built what magic always built—some sort of sigil- and sign-based gearwork structure. Except…

I stood and showed her the photo. "Here," I drew my finger up and outward. "And here." I moved my finger again, but in the opposite direction. "Looks like a tree."

It looked like the ash on the side of my head. "The world tree is not a symbol of death," I said.

She touched her lips.

"The enchantments may have hurt you, but I don't think the tree would show if someone died," I said.

Her friend was okay.

Ellie hugged me. She curled her arms around my waist and pressed her face against my chest. She touched me and did not recoil from my cold flesh.

"Thank you," she said.

And again, I wanted to pick her up. I wanted to make sure she understood that neither Marcus Aurelius nor I would forget her. That come tomorrow, we would both remember.

"Would you like to get some coffee?" I pointed toward town. "There's a place called Lara's Café not far from here. You can tell me about your friend."

She looked away. "You won't remember me tomorrow."

4

Yes, I will, I thought. "If I don't, Marcus Aurelius will remind me, won't you, boy?"

My dog emperor barked.

"I'd like to learn about your friend," I said. I wanted to learn about her, to help me remember.

She extended her hand.

No fear radiated off her body. Her magic twisted and wavered like silk in a breeze. Hope had returned to her eyes.

She offered me a touch.

I curled my palm around her fingers. "Come, Ellie Jones." I bowed. "The emperor and I will keep you company until we can no more," I said.

I would break the enchantments hiding her from the world. No matter what happened—even if she decided I was too cold or too large or too ugly. Even if we spent the rest of our days as only friends.

I would do my best.

CHAPTER 2

I fell for a woman once, long ago. An elf. She still lived in Alfheim.

We don't talk.

Ellie rolled down the passenger window of my truck and closed her eyes. She faced the breeze as if she'd never ridden in an automobile before.

Marcus Aurelius poked his head between the seats.

She laughed and scratched his ears. "Did I take your spot?" she asked my dog.

My big dog—Marcus Aurelius outweighed my eight-year-old elf-niece, Akeyla—whimpered and tried to crawl over the gearshift and onto Ellie's lap.

"Hey, hey." I put my hand out. "You're too big for that." My truck was big, too—at almost seven feet tall, I find driving a sedan not only uncomfortable but nearly impossible—but the cab only had so much room.

Marcus Aurelius whimpered again and settled for rubbing his big golden head against Ellie's elbow.

"So you think a cell phone might bypass the enchantments?" she asked. A bag with her new phone sat on the floor between her feet. I'd added her to my plan at the store and picked up a nice unit with lots of memory for photos and videos for her to use.

There'd been a small argument. We'd just met and having a man she didn't know hand her a new cell phone raised her hackles. But we both understood that because of the enchantments, she couldn't hold a contract. Plus, her line showing up on my bill might be enough to cut through the fog and help me to remember.

So she let me set her up. She didn't have to use it if she didn't want to, but at least she had access now, in case of an emergency.

I added my number, and Ed's, and Axlam Geroux's after I texted her and asked if it was okay. As one of the Alfheim Pack's Alphas, Axlam understood helping skittish people for whom magic had laid down a blister. She'd agreed immediately and without a lot of explanation.

Many magicals found werewolves too volatile and worked toward their eradication, but to Alfheim, the pack was a blessing.

Ellie spent a lot of time staring at the phone in the bag.

"It's worth a try." I'd lost my phone the night before chasing down my murderous vampire brother. All Ellie knew so far was that I'd been involved in a vampire-caused emergency and that it was now under control.

Mostly under control. We still did not know where Alfheim's two local vampires had gone, or if the "brother" creature my arrogant father had built out of vampire parts was dead or hiding in the underbrush somewhere in the forest.

Not that I was hiding information from Ellie. She hadn't asked for specifics, and right now, seeing her happy about maybe bypassing her concealment enchantments trumped any need to bring her up-to-date on her new home's magical particulars.

And Alfheim was most definitely her new home. Seemed that not only did magic toss her into a new location, it also moved her cottage. Actually, physically moved her and her home from one location to another. Yesterday she'd woken up in Tokyo; last night she'd fallen asleep in a meadow under a Minnesota sky.

I signaled and pulled the truck onto the road leading toward one of Alfheim's mainstays—Lara's Café. The restaurant itself might be boarded up while they fixed the damage from the explosion, but the owners had pulled their food truck around front, serving fritters and coffee.

I glanced over just as Ellie pushed a strand of hair off her forehead. Her skin glowed in the morning light—she wasn't quite as pale as an elf, but she did look as if she carried northern European ancestry. Mostly, with her hair and her green eyes, she looked Irish to me. Irish in that she carried bits of all who had come to the Isle—the original Gaelic plus a touch of the Norse and some Anglo-Saxon mixed in.

Ellie Jones, a woman of the Isles, and the seer who used Victorian-era daguerreotype photos as her stone.

I had so many questions.

She lifted her chin and inhaled the fresh Minnesota breeze. "Chihiro tried saving photos on her phone," she said.

Chihiro, the friend she'd left behind in Tokyo—and the friend who had figured out how to at least somewhat bypass the enchantments. Ellie was not sure how. But Chihiro was proof bypassing was possible.

Marcus Aurelius nudged Ellie's elbow. She laughed and rubbed his head.

She really was beautiful.

I returned my attention to the road. Best not to be distracted and get us into an accident.

I would talk to Ed Martinez—Alfheim's sheriff—to see if we could track down Chihiro. It would be a good test of the boundaries of Ellie's concealment enchantments, and a nice surprise for her if it worked out.

"Did it help?" I asked.

Ellie frowned. "You know, I'm not sure." Her frown deepened. "Sometimes I think the enchantments conceal parts of my life from me as well as concealing me from the world."

Not good, I thought. When she told me that the enchantments were layered, I figured she meant in the outward progression the way most complicated magicks built upon each other. A spell that warped Ellie's memories in a different way added a whole new level of intricacy to a gearwork that was already much more intense than any I'd seen an elf produce.

And all this without leaving obvious traces of magic around its primary target.

Only natural-looking wisps of magic flittered around Ellie. They reminded me of the inborn, normal hints that surrounded all of the elves and the born-wolf werewolves. The wisps weren't controlled magic, but a hint that magic was controllable for the person they surrounded.

The elves could often tell if someone was magical with a first impression, even though they did not see magic the way I did. Dagrun Tyrsdottir—Alfheim's Queen—once told me that she "felt" magic when it moved along her own, like silk touching silk. I see that "silk."

Only Ellie's natural magic floated around her. No designed spells. No shifting, twisting enchantments. No sigils in the air and most definitely no tattooed, gifted tracers or protections such as the ones I carried.

So the intricate, layered spellwork that hid Ellie from the world was not centered on her person, even if it affected her personally, which meant a level of enchantment-weaving that outstripped any and all I had ever come across. Whoever had cast the concealments might very well be able to take on all of Alfheim and win.

Only a fae could out-magic the elves, and then only a powerful one.

"We're going to put an end to the concealment enchantments messing with your life," I said. "Right, boy?"

Marcus Aurelius barked.

"See? The emperor agrees."

Ellie laughed. "Thank you," she said. "Both of you." But she didn't seem convinced.

I wasn't convinced. Who was I to think I could help her figure out this puzzle? I was just a man. A re-animated, patchwork man, and one who wasn't inherently magical.

I glanced at Ellie again. All evidence with her enchantments pointed to the involvement of a high-born fae, and high-born fae were not... nice. The fae were basically primal elves—magicals more removed from the mundanes, more elemental, and less caring. Arne Odinsson once told me that the elves, the kami, and the fae were like orcas—they were all the same "species" but some lived in transient pods unconnected from places.

The fae were transient in the world. They came and went, and were not as much of the land as the elves or the kami.

Never in my two centuries had I come across an actual fae in person. But I'd seen and felt their effects.

What was happening to Ellie was definitely fae-generated.

And no elf in Alfheim would dare take on a powerful fae. Not our leaders, Arne and Dagrun. They had too much to lose. Not our more loud and bombastic elves who revel in annoying both magicals and mundanes alike.

I grinned for Ellie. "We will figure out what needs figuring."

She laughed again. "All in one day?"

I pulled the truck into the parking lot of Lara's Café. The explosion a few days ago blew out the restaurant's kitchen and window. The morning sun reflected off the plywood over the hole and added an extra sunny glow to the tables dotting the open area in front of the building.

Lara's food truck sat in the front lot, and the owners were serving their normal morning coffee and pastries from the service counter on the side. The scent of caramel dominated the blueberry and apple of their popovers, and filled the entire lot with a mouthwatering warmth. Today, a hint of pumpkin mixed in from this morning's special muffins.

All of Alfheim seemed to be pulling into the lot to support their favorite local restaurant, which was nice to see.

Tomorrow, I would at least remember the community coming together, even if I didn't remember Ellie.

She stared at Lara's huge green, purple, and red truck and its painted-on "Voted Best Duluth International Food Festival Vendor" emblem. "This place is a lot different from Tokyo," she said.

I chuckled. "It's a lot different from Duluth, and that's about two hours east of here."

"See," she pointed at my nose. "No one in Japan measures distance in hours traveled."

I'd never thought about it, but it did seem to be a cultural feature of areas where traveling took up a lot of a person's time. "Welcome to Minnesota," I said.

She inhaled. "Smells good."

"The coffee is excellent." I pulled my door handle. "I'll get you a welcome muffin."

She reached for her handle, but stopped and pulled the photo plate out of her hoodie's pocket. Slowly, she ran her finger over the sigil decorating the protective sleeve.

I realized I couldn't identify the sleeve's material, and I'd handled it. Was it leather? A stiff fabric? Woven bamboo? Whatever it was, it had a slight sheen.

I couldn't even tell its true color.

Ellie set the sleeve and the plate it protected inside the bag with her new phone. "Is it okay if I leave this in your truck?" she asked.

"It's not a problem," I said, though that sleeve obviously had its own enchantment. I pointed at it. "I don't see any magic around the plate."

"Oh," she said. She touched it again. "It's localized to the photo. I bet if you hold it up and look at it on edge, you'll see the spells I use to develop it."

Which I shouldn't do out here in the open, in front of mundanes, in the parking lot of Lara's Café. "I look forward to it."

Ellie smiled.

I had to figure out how to remember her. Not helping her was going to burn a hole in my life. Not remembering that smile was going to slash at my soul.

She looked away and tucked another stray strand of hair behind her ear.

The flirting was killing me. Not that I wasn't already semi-dead— my father built me from the parts of others. But I'd spent two-hundred-plus years with my bits and pieces growing together to become me, and what life I had was my own.

But women found waking up next to morning-cold me to be unpleasant. Not that Ellie would be waking next to me. Not with the enchantments that would make sure that tomorrow morning, we would meet again anew.

And, I suspected, I would once again find myself flirting with a beautiful woman about whom I shouldn't—and couldn't—get my hopes up.

Ellie pulled her handle as she nodded over her shoulder at the boarded-up front window, then over her other shoulder at the food truck parked in the lot. "What happened?"

She carefully swung out her legs. Her limp hadn't let up, and her thigh obviously still hurt. But nothing seemed broken.

Marcus Aurelius bounded out after Ellie, gleefully wagging his tail as he walked at her slowly-moving side toward Lara's food truck.

I'd offer my arm but my dog had the situation under control. "A vampire," I said. "He blew out the café's kitchen and seating area."

"The same vampire who burned down your neighbor's house?" Ellie rubbed Marcus Aurelius's head as they walked toward the truck.

Three customers laughed and chattered as the owner handed over coffee and pastries. I recognized one—Mark Ellis from the Alfheim Pack—and waved as he and his friends made their way toward the tables.

"Hi, Frank!" Mark called. He nodded to Ellie and shot me a "Well done, my friend" look when she turned her attention to the truck's menu.

I frowned and shook my head. Mark chuckled. "Later!" he said, and sat next to his buddies.

Ellie looked up at my face when I stopped next to her side. "Same suspect, yes," I said.

She opened her mouth, then closed it as she took in the mundanes ordering coffee. "Well, I hope they catch him. It's not good having a firebug around."

"True," I said.

She motioned toward Mark and his friends. "Your friend..." She waited until the mundanes walked away. "He's a..." She squinted and tilted her head. "... a wolf?"

She could tell?

"The other two are mundane." She returned her attention to the menu. "I can't *see*, if that's what you're wondering. Not without my camera obscura and a plate." She leaned close. "But you get a feel for your subjects, you know? It's an educated guess based on body language."

I looked back at Mark. In his human form, he walked and moved like any other person.

Ellie smiled. "Maybe someday we'll have time and I can teach you."

If I didn't figure out her concealment enchantments, all the flirting would kill me each day.

Ellie stepped up to the window and placed her order. I placed mine and paid. We stepped away, muffins and coffee in hand, plus a cup of whipped cream for the emperor, and walked toward the truck.

"Thank you for breakfast," she said. "And the phone." She set her muffin on the hood, then set the cream on the ground for Marcus Aurelius. "And the company."

I also set my coffee and muffin on the hood. "Picture time," I said, and pulled out my phone.

Ellie didn't smile. Sadness continued to permeate her expression, but she did snuggle up to Marcus Aurelius.

No way I would forget her now. Not with a picture like the one I just took.

I pulled up my note-taking app and held out my phone. "Any information you remember about your friend would be appreciated."

She blinked. "Why?"

"I'm going to find her for you. Make sure she's okay."

Ellie stared at me for a long moment. "Really?"

I hadn't expected surprise. "Yes," I answered.

Ellie reached for my phone just as a Sheriff's Department cruiser pulled into the lot.

Eduardo Martinez, our vampire-slaying town sheriff. He rolled down his window. "Frank!" he called, and waved me over.

A bad feeling poked at my gut, and it wasn't the muffin. From the expression on Ed's face, I could tell he had information on my vampiric brother.

I looked at Ellie. "Go on," she said, and continued to tap at my phone.

I nodded, and walked toward Ed.

CHAPTER 3

Ed Martinez dropped his hat through his cruiser's open window. He rubbed his stubbly head and watched Lara's truck as if he was the vampire and caffeine was his blood of choice.

Then he leaned against the cruiser's door and nodded toward Ellie. "Who's the woman?" he asked.

"Her name is Ellie Jones," I said. "Marcus Aurelius found her and brought her down to the lake."

"Good to hear your dog came home." Ed sniffed and reached for his notebook.

"I found him—them—this morning."

Ed flipped open his book. "She's a hiker? I don't recognize her. No missing persons reports have come in."

I sipped at my coffee. "She's new in town."

"Hmm." Ed watched Ellie. "You're having breakfast with a lady the morning after we dealt with a monster?" He sounded more amused than I expected.

Ellie glanced over. She smiled and waved.

Ed chuckled. "Town newbie, huh?" Ed knew what "new" meant. He tucked his notebook back into his pocket. He never took notes when magic was involved.

Should I tell him about the magic involved? I should, but then again, Ed had enough to worry about with the vampires. "Any word on the Bitersons?" I didn't ask about my brother.

Ed rubbed his face. "No." He rubbed it again. "I'm on my way home, by the way. Spent most of the night out looking for anything suspicious."

"I take it the pack didn't find anything."

Ed shook his head. "Gerard and Remy think your brother might have *poofed* into a cloud of dust." He spread out his fingers to sign an explosion. "Doubtful," he said.

Gerard and Remy Geroux were the Alfheim Pack's other two Alphas. "Yeah," I said. "When has anyone ever been that lucky when dealing with vampires?"

Ed pointed at the hamburger-like scar on his neck. "I got damned lucky that vamp in Texas only left me with this."

Arne Odinsson and the Geroux brothers had gone down to Texas thinking they were dealing with a rogue werewolf. Turned out to be a vampire serial killer. Ed and his family were now in Alfheim partly to protect them from Gulf Coast vampire clans.

The clans stayed out of Minnesota, nor did they set foot in Iceland or Norway because of the elves. The Siberian elves have had some issues, mostly because the old-guard Eastern European vampires tended to be meaner, more violent, and significantly smarter than the rest of the world's bloodsuckers.

Except the handful of Japanese vampires. From the stories I'd heard, the Japanese vamps made even the Romanians quake in their boots.

I glanced at Ellie. She smiled again and waved my phone as if she'd finished adding the information about her friend and wanted to share.

"Listen," Ed said. "I want you to go out with a couple of elves this morning, okay? Take a fresh pair of pointy ears and go sniffing for Biterson stink." He sighed. "We had five calls last night about missing animals. Five, Frank. A stablehand at Magnus's place found one of their dogs ripped apart this morning. It was not a wolf. They were all accounted for last night."

Magnus Freyrsson was one of Alfheim's founding fathers. He crossed the Atlantic with Arne Odinsson and was one of the handful of remaining original elves. Magnus was also the most mundanely successful elf in town. He owned trucking companies, car and truck dealerships, and a breeding operation outside of town that was mostly a cover for stabling Alfheim's elven mounts.

All of Magnus's horses were special, even his bred-for-the-mundanes animals. Over the years, all of my horses had come from Magnus. I think he enjoyed the challenge of breeding a mount appropriate for my size and strength.

"That's not all," Ed said.

What else could have happened? "His horses are okay?" I asked.

Ed shook his head. "Something spooked the entire herd pretty bad last night. Several ran off. A couple of their fences are down, too." He rubbed his face. "Almost a million dollars' worth of prime, prize-winning equine stock was still unaccounted for when they called it in this morning."

Vampires would eat a horse, not steal one. "Damn," I said.

Usually. But then again, my brother was not a usual vampire.

Ed stared at the people ordering from the truck. "The best case scenario is Magnus's people find his horses in someone else's pasture." His fatigue slowed just about everything—his words, blinks, thinking.

I waited.

He looked up at me. "We do not need a distraction."

"I agree."

He continued to watch the mundanes of Alfheim order their morning coffee. "Thank God our problem isn't going after people. Yet."

Feral vampires always escalated. Always. They were of two souls— one the human vessel and the other the vampiric demon who reformed their flesh. The demon could be controlled, but only if the human was strong-willed and had help.

The Bitersons used to have help from the elves. No longer. Finding them had to be a priority.

17

"Who do you have in mind?" The better trackers had gone out with the wolves for the full moon and were likely as tired as Ed.

He shrugged. "Ask Arne or Dag." This time, he rubbed his neck. "I'll go back out this afternoon."

"Sure. No problem." I'd have to take Ellie home. Exposing her to possible vampires wasn't a good idea.

I'd promised her time to talk about her friend and her life. I'd wanted to give her at least some connection here.

Ed moved to open his door.

"Hey," I said. "Could I ask a favor?"

Ed stopped and looked up at me. "What?"

His fatigue was making him terse. Perhaps I should ask some other time. But then again, I might not remember to do the asking.

I waved Ellie over. "Ellie," I said, "this is Ed Martinez, Alfheim's sheriff. Ed, meet Ellie Jones."

They shook hands. "Hello," Ellie said. "Frank put your number in my new phone." She pointed at the truck at the same time she handed me my phone.

"Ed knows about magic," I said.

"Ah," Ellie said. "I'm a seer." She left it at that.

Ed did not look impressed—or happy—probably because "seer" often meant "witch." And "witch" meant problems.

But he kept his unease to himself, most likely because of his exhaustion. "Nice to meet you," he said. He glanced at her leg, but didn't ask about her limp.

I pulled up the information about her friend. "Chihiro Hatanaka" it said. I forwarded it to Ed. "Would you check if there've been any reports concerning this woman? She's a Japanese national living in Tokyo."

Ed frowned. "I'm not Interpol, Frank." he said.

His fatigue had pushed him through terse into argumentative. I couldn't blame him, especially with the horse thief issue. He really did not need extra distractions. But I needed to ask now, before the inevitable happened and I did not remember tomorrow.

"If you get a chance. We'd appreciate it."

Ellie threw him one of her lovely smiles.

Ed grumbled something about not holding my breath.

"Are you okay to drive?" I asked.

He rolled his eyes. "Go talk to Dag. They're all at home this morning. Maura is up there, too."

"Will do." It'd be good to talk to Maura and see how she and Akeyla were faring after last night's vampire adventures. Ed nodded to Ellie again. "Welcome to Alfheim," he said, and ducked into his cruiser.

"I hope he gets some sleep," Ellie said as she watched Ed pull away.

I watched him go. I couldn't take Ellie near the elf enclave in the River District. She'd said something about not being welcomed by elves, so best not to add yet another possibility for misunderstanding onto a day already full of issues.

"Are the concealment enchantments moment-to-moment?" I asked. "If I take you home, will I remember to come by later this afternoon?"

She tucked her hands into the pocket of her hoodie. "The enchantments seem to do their cleansing overnight. At least that's what happened with Chihiro."

"And here we were going to have a nice conversation about Tokyo and your friend," I said. She needed to talk. That was obvious. Solitude is fine, if that's what you want. But isolation was not, and nothing forced someone into isolation faster than concealment enchantments that robbed potential friends of their memories.

"I'll be okay," she said. "I don't usually leave my cottage this soon after a move anyway." She inhaled and stood up straight. "Thank you for your help."

"I have a lot of questions about how the enchantments work," I said.

Ellie stepped closer. She stopped well within my personal space—most people give me a good three or more feet, I suspect mostly because my shoulders tend to throw a wide shadow. But Ellie stood close enough I could easily pull her in for a hug.

I almost did.

We'd just met. We did not know each other. And here I was feeling like the enchanted one.

She touched my arm. "I think we have a connection. I have faith, Mr. Victorsson." She nodded over her shoulder at my dog, who sat next to my truck. "I blame Marcus Aurelius."

I chuckled. "He *is* the emperor. We must comply."

Ellie laughed. "Tell you what. I'll check my library for anything on vampires." She stepped back and stuck her hands in her pocket again, and her expression took on the same perplexed twist it had when she told me that sometimes she wondered if the enchantments stole her memories, as well. "My cottage moves, and the garden changes, but I think the library stays the same."

She looked up at me. "If you find something you can't read while you're out looking, I can use my camera."

She was offering to use her seer ability to help us find the vampires.

"Thank you," I said.

"Can we get a couple more muffins before we leave?"

I'd buy her the entire truck, if I could. "Does that cottage of yours feed you? Do you need groceries?" I pointed into town.

Ellie gave me a quick hug. Her arms wrapped around my waist and for a singular, glorious moment, she pressed up against my abdomen and chest.

I bowed my head and inhaled the sweet, lavender scent of her hair as I did my damnedest not to engulf her like some massive, swooping monster.

She pulled away, but not too far, and tipped her head to the side when she looked up at my face. Her expression showed concern. Concentration. Ellie, it seemed, was as unsure about the connection we shared as I was.

"Are you sure you just landed here?" I asked.

Her hand rose and for a second, she held her palm up. Then she touched my chest.

Over the two centuries of my lifetime, through my many decades,

I've learned to deal with the hand dealt me by my rebirth. The scars. The frightening physical size. The lumbering. The cold flesh.

I am not now, nor have I ever been, beautiful. And my lack of beauty has woven its own concealment enchantment around my life.

Solitude is fine; isolation is not. I know this firsthand. And right now, right here in the lot of Lara's Café, the most perfect woman I have ever met reached through the isolation spell of my existence and placed her hand on my chest.

I learned a long time ago not to get my hopes up. The higher the hopes, the more broken my bones when my emotions pushed me over that ledge.

"I'm sure," she said. She looked away when Marcus Aurelius trotted over. "I'll be fine at home." She rubbed his head.

"Maybe the emperor could spend the day with you." I could use his help tracking, but something told me he'd run off again because, like me, he would rather spend the day with Ellie than poking through the brush looking for vampire scat.

"I'd like that," she said, and took my hand. "Let's get those muffins."

CHAPTER 4

W e stopped at my place to pick up food for Marcus Aurelius. Ellie stood on my deck staring at the Carlsons' burned-down glass-and-chrome home across the lake.

She hitched up the backpack I'd loaded with dog chow, tea, and paper towels onto her shoulder. "The vampire did that?" she asked.

The birds sang and the lake lapped, but the stink of fried electricals and insulation still wafted over the lake. "A fire elf started the fire and chased off the vampire," I said. "We're not sure if he survived."

"You need to find him," she said, then looked up at my face. "In the daylight, okay?" Her eyebrows pulled together.

I wasn't used to a woman other than my adoptive sister and mother showing concern. "I'll be careful."

Ellie closed her eyes and tilted her head as if listening to the world whisper. "I think I'll walk home," she said. "It will help me get a sense of the land."

Even with vampires around? I thought, but it was day, and we weren't dealing with day-walkers. Not really. Not outside the elf glamours.

And she was still limping. "Are you sure?" I stepped closer and pointed at her thigh. "I can drive you. It's not a problem."

She squeezed my hand. "I'm not sure you can get your truck near the cottage." She frowned again, the same way she'd frowned when she couldn't quite remember if taking photos with her cell phone had helped her friend remember.

There were clues here. Instances to which I needed to attend. But I had no way of pushing my attention to those clues into the next day.

Damned concealment enchantments.

Ellie slapped her undamaged thigh. "Do you want to keep me company today, or do you want to chase vampires?" she asked Marcus Aurelius.

He wagged his tail and pressed against her hurt leg. "Careful," she said, then caught herself. "The bruise isn't that bad," she said. "I can walk."

I didn't argue, and rubbed my dog's neck. "Watch for the bad things," I said.

He barked his response.

Ellie gingerly stepped off the deck onto the path around my house. She gripped a large stick, peered into the trees, then looked over her shoulder at me. "I'll tell you about Chihiro another time," she said.

She walked into the woods, my dog beside her, and made her way toward her enchanted home.

I couldn't shake the feeling that I'd just allowed her concealment enchantments to reset. That come this evening or tomorrow, or whenever I saw her again, we would be starting from scratch, and that the obvious would always be new and not obvious at all.

Next time Ed wanted me to abandon Ellie, I was going to say no. I didn't care if vampires blotted out the sun and were turning all the mundanes of Alfheim. I'd set the edges of the jigsaw puzzle that was Ellie Jones—gotten the corner pieces where they were supposed to be, and sorted out some of the patterns. Watching her walk away felt like someone had just tossed that puzzle into the air.

I watched them vanish into the trees.

I pulled out my phone and dialed Dag's number.

"Frank," she said when she answered.

"I'm leaving my place now," I said.

23

"Good." Then the Queen of Alfheim hung up on me.

The elves did not approve of cell phones. I can't say I blamed them.

I stared at my phone's screen, then looked out at the trees again. A few swipes later, my photo of Ellie hugging Marcus Aurelius was my new background.

A strand of her auburn hair stuck to her cheek, and she looked out at me with her light-colored eyes. Were they blue? Green? Somewhere in between? I couldn't remember.

I scowled and tucked the phone back into my pocket. For Ellie's safety—and for mine, and the town's as well—I needed a definitive accounting of my brother's demise. And I needed to make sure the Bitersons weren't about to go human-eating feral.

I closed the French doors leading to the deck and made my way to my truck.

From the outside, the River District looked like an enclave of turn-of-the-century homes. Most medium-sized Minnesota towns had an area with large, impressive houses built when logging and milling made for a robust resource-consuming economy.

The houses here weren't as ostentatious as the grand homes in Minneapolis and St. Paul, nor were they the behemoths built by the wealthy of St. Louis and New Orleans. But they were lovely and large, and even though most were stone and brick, they carried the steeply-pitched roofs and the overall lines of Scandinavian architecture that the elves preferred.

Dag and Arne's house stood on its own hill, surrounded by a larger walled garden than most of the other homes. Trees blocked the view of the front of the building. Wildflowers and native plants grew between the thick, brick garden wall and the sidewalk. When I pulled up, a wild turkey tom gobbled as he darted out and down the road.

I parked and pulled the key from the ignition. The River District, like every place the elves walked, smelled fresher than the town's regular air.

The birds sang louder here, too. A few trees over, a male cardinal chirped out a call to his mate. A rabbit hopped through the wildflower area in front of Dag and Arne's house, and stopped to munch on the native grass.

The houses were built on solid non-magical foundations, and the elves glamoured very little of their homes' surroundings. The trees shimmered and rustled, but more because the land here was managed better than other areas of town than because of any magic.

Waves and wisps of spells still floated up off the plants. Nature made its own magic, and when elves claimed a spot, that natural magic went into overdrive.

I closed the truck's door and walked toward Alfheim's default castle.

Arne had lived on these lands for a millennium; Dag had come over from Iceland in the Seventeenth Century as part of the elves' attempts to reconnect their far-flung communities. In reality, Dag's father married her off to Arne to pull the North American elves back into the fold.

Such was the way of royalty, mundane and elven alike.

Their house wasn't massive. It did have a covered drive under which a horse carriage once stopped, and an outbuilding that used to serve as a stable. Now Arne and Dag kept their horses at Magnus's operation, and the house's former stable now kept Arne's econo-vehicle and Dag's dusty-blue roadster.

Sometimes an elf or two would live above the garage, but the apartment seemed to be empty right now.

The house itself was built from locally-sourced oaks and purplish locally-quarried basalt. The building was a strong four-square home with five bedrooms and a fireplace in every room, but the front door stole my attention every time I visited.

Not many thresholds were tall and wide enough that I felt comfortable walking straight through, but I could here. The massive ash double doors stood ten feet tall, and together, seven feet wide.

Yggdrasil, the world tree, coiled and curled across the two doors. Norse runes and symbols wove through the branches, as did the requisite animals: an eagle, a squirrel, two ravens, a stag, and a snake at the roots.

Every time I came to Arne and Dag's home, I symbolically touched the entire universe.

I knocked.

Stomping echoed from inside, then a small head peeked out behind the glass next to the door. A squeal followed and the door unlocked.

I pushed it open.

Akeyla hugged my leg. "Uncle Frank!" she squealed again. Her flickering fire magic danced around her eight-year-old body as she reached out for me to lift her up.

Her glamour sputtered a bit—not a lot, but enough so I noticed. I doubted a mundane person would see, but every so often, a mirage of her tall, pointed elf ears flickered like moving shadows next to her head. "Are you doing okay, pumpkin?"

She was too big for most everyone else to carry, though Arne had the strength to hold her when she needed an adult to help her calm down or hold her glamour, so me swirling her around was always a treat.

I carefully hoisted her onto my hip. "How's your head?" I asked. She'd gotten a good knock last night, not to mention breathing smoke from the fire. But she was Akeyla Maurasdottir, half-elf, half-fire-spirit, and if anyone could come out of a burning house okay, it would be my eight-year-old adoptive niece.

She rubbed her ear. "My head hurts. Mommy said I can stay home from school tomorrow and maybe the day after but I can't miss the whole week." She hugged my neck. "Jax got to stay home today too, but his mommy wouldn't let him come over so we've been chatting on my phone." She wiggled her thumbs.

I wasn't surprised Axlam kept Jaxson home, as well. Both kids had stood up to a terrifying vampire. Who knew what sort of traumatic aftereffects they might suffer? But other than the headache, Akeyla seemed fine.

I carried her through the foyer and into the wide hallway leading toward the kitchen at the back of the house. "Where's your grandmother?"

Akeyla sniffed. "Yelling at grandpa," she said. "Mommy goes in and tells them to be quiet but they start yelling again."

Was I surprised? Dag had had her fill of medieval elven political proclamations and wasn't about to send Maura and Akeyla back to Hawaii. Arne had finally agreed after my brother vanished.

The big oak door to Arne's study flew open. Angry Icelandic words followed, then Dag stepped out into the hallway.

Unlike Akeyla, she was fully out of her glamour.

Dagrun Tyrsdottir stood barefoot on the wood flooring in an elven gown of softness and light. Magic wrapped around her body and gave life to the linen sheath she wore. The dress responded to the curves of her breasts and hips as if alive. Her ears seemed taller this morning as well, and her black ponytail as alive as her magic.

Anger made an already glorious elf all the more magnificent. And like her daughter—like all the elves—Dag was an unearthly beauty who, even to this day, took my breath away.

But she was also my adoptive mother, and her arm was still in a sling. She'd damaged herself deeply holding back the fire so I could carry Akeyla out.

She waved her good hand at me. "Maura needs to recuperate, as do I." Then she frowned over her shoulder. "My husband will tell you that he rubbed a poultice on his wounds and thus is in fine fighting shape."

I'd seen the rip in his leg. Arne needed recovery time, too.

Dag returned her gaze to me. "That mundane lawyer? Aaron Carlson."

The owner of the now-burned-down house across the lake. "Yes," I said.

Dag's brow cinched. "He is asking too many questions." She sighed. "Plus the international politics have now also expanded to include the Siberians."

"Santa lives in Siberia!" Akeyla said.

Whether or not an actual jolly old elf named Santa lived in the

Siberian enclave, I did not know. What I did know was that they tended to take up a lot of Arne's time when something caught their attention—which meant that Arne would be staying here, "poultice on his wounds" or not.

"Ed asked me to take a good tracker out into the woods," I said.

Dag was the best tracker Alfheim had, but she was wounded. Maura had a talent for it, but not the experience. The three other elves in Alfheim who topped my list were also the three Arne routinely called in to run with the wolves at full moon, and all three of them had been out last night.

Which limited my choices of powerful, experienced elves.

Of the other remaining town elders, Magnus also had his hands full today, and the other no one bothered.

Thirty elves had come with Dag from Iceland in the sixteen hundreds. Most have passed. One returned home in the eighteen hundreds, and another went to the Norwegians. Other than Dag, only two still lived in Alfheim.

One did not track well. The other, I no longer talked to.

Dag rubbed her wounded shoulder. "I called Benta."

Who else would she have called? Benta the Nameless was almost as good a tracker as Dag herself. And if there was anyone in Alfheim who could charm a raging vampire to his knees, it was Benta.

She'd charmed me, long ago.

Damn it, I thought. So much for not talking to her.

"It's been a century, Frank." Dag sounded like the adoptive mother she was.

Benta and I had a couple of good years after Rose's death. She'd taken pity on my poor, tortured soul. Then when the contortions of my torture became too much, she walked away from my cold, stiff body.

But Benta was Dag's friend. She was also arguably as powerful, even though she used her magicks more in service of the animals of the world than of the elves. She ran a small sanctuary outside of town and specialized in rehabilitating cougars, lynxes, and bobcats so they could be released into their natural habitats.

Benta could track any animal anywhere.

Yes, it had been a century, but we did not end well. "I don't have her number," I said.

Dag motioned toward the study. "Where do you want her to meet you? I will have her call you."

Where? I thought. Where could I handle a face-to-face with the elf who I once thought was the love of my life?

"Rose's Hill," I answered. The place where I first came face-to-face with my brother.

And also the place where Benta cut out my heart.

Dag frowned. "Akeyla, honey, will you go check on your mommy for me? She needs to eat breakfast."

Akeyla wiggled out of my arms and stood tall when I set her down. "Okay, Grandma," she said, then walked slowly down the hall toward the back stairs.

Dag watched her go. "She is healing faster than the rest of us," she said.

"I'll track him, Dag. Don't worry."

She returned her gaze to me and walked over. "I know," she said. She touched my elbow, and her body relaxed a bit. "The axe has been asking about you."

She'd semi-gifted me an elven battle axe for my fight against my brother. Turned out that the axe—and the wooden dagger which Rose had gifted me—were what I could only describe as "magically conscious." They were objects, not living things, but the magic they carried reacted to the world as if they were alive. And it seemed the axe had taken a shine to me.

"We can't make Benta jealous, now can we?" My tone sounded harsher to my ears than I meant, and once the words settled, I realized that they too were harsh.

Dag lifted her hand off my arm. She sighed yet again and stared down the hallway, obviously choosing to let my comment slide. "I cannot accommodate you with the axe right now." She pointed at her damaged elbow. "My magicks need the same recuperation I do."

They did. The gearwork of her magical armor looked slower than I was used to, and slightly out of focus. "You need sleep," I said.

She sniffed. "I will have someone bring the axe out to your truck." She stepped away. "In case Benta needs it." But she stopped and her eyes narrowed. She tipped her head toward the den as if listening. Then she frowned yet again. "Wait outside," she said, and walked away toward the back of the house.

I turned toward the front door and did my best to follow the orders of the Elf Queen of Alfheim.

CHAPTER 5

It dawned on me, as I leaned against my truck and waited for the delivery of my friend the elven axe, that I should have asked Dag about concealment enchantments.

I'd completely forgotten.

The house's side door opened and my attention shifted to Maura as she carried the glamoured axe out of the house. She held it on her shoulder like a lumberjack—the axe looked like a wood-chopping axe—and walked less gracefully toward my truck than an elf should.

Maura and Akeyla used to live at my place. They still did, unless Arne decreed that they had to move back into the main house. I hoped not. I liked having Akeyla around.

I stood up straight. Maura stopped at the tailgate with one hand on the axe handle and the other on her hip. She wore her usual glamour —"Akeyla's Mom" she called it, but to me she looked like every other beautiful woman walking around Alfheim.

"Mom says the axe likes you." She grinned. "It doesn't really talk to me." She flipped it off her shoulder and held it in both hands. "If you're going to wield it again, Mom says you'll need to have Benta make you gloves."

Great, I thought.

Maura hopped up into the back of the truck and made her way to the toolbox. "Got a blanket I can wrap this in?" she asked.

I got the distinct impression that the axe didn't want to be wrapped up in a blanket. "I think it wants to socialize with the other tools," I said.

Maura looked over the side of the truck. "Seriously?" She swirled it between her hands like a baton. "The axe wants to have a deep-felt conversation with your tape measure?"

"Magic works in mysterious ways," I said. The axe agreed.

Maura set it in the box, closed the lid, and shrugged as she wiped her hands on her pants. "Who are we to disagree with magic?" she said.

I helped her off the back of the truck. "Thank you for bringing it out."

"No problem," she said. "Hey," she pointed toward the truck, "are you okay with us moving back in?"

As far as I was concerned, Maura and Akeyla had never moved out. "My house is your house."

Maura gave me a quick hug. "This weekend, then, I think." She stared at her parents' home for a long moment. "We'll come back once I know Mom's okay."

"My brother did a number on her arm." He'd smashed her elbow to the point she needed the cast and sling for a couple of weeks, which, for an elf, was an eternity.

"It's not that," Maura said. "It's the politics."

Maura's almost-banishment. Dag's unmovable Icelandic-Elf-Emperor father. And most likely, the yelling Akeyla mentioned.

"Dad knows he's going to have a fight on his hands if he doesn't stand up to the other kings." Maura looked up at me. "We're staying in Alfheim. You don't have to worry." Then back at the house.

I squeezed Maura's shoulder. "If it gets too bad, bring your mom, too."

Maura chuckled. "Dad will kick you out of town for stealing his women."

That was me, the walking corpse who charmed elves. I shook my head.

She patted my arm. "You are way too hard on yourself, big brother." She touched the side of her nose then pointed at me as she walked back toward the house. "Mom already called Benta. She'll meet you at Rose's Hill."

I dug my keys out of my pocket.

"Keep it civil!"

Once again I shook my head. "I will," I called, knowing full well that the civil part would be more in Benta's corner than my own.

Mostly.

I got into my truck and drove toward Rose's Hill.

MY ADOPTED daughter had been a witch, and when the witchiness took her mind, she set fire to her cottage, herself, and one of Arne's most powerful lieutenants.

Rose Franksdottir didn't mean to take an elder elf with her into The Land of the Dead, but she had. The elf tried to help her, to stop the disintegration of her mind, but some ragings will run their course no matter the dams you place in their way.

So witches were not welcome in Alfheim.

I stopped my truck at the base of the hill on which Rose's cottage once sat. Nothing remained beyond the stone hearth. Arne destroyed what was left of her papers last week, in a fit of his own rage.

The same fit that sent the Biterson brothers into hiding.

I looked up through the trees at the hill. Seers were witches.

I swore and slapped my steering wheel. I'd forgotten to ask Maura about Ellie's concealment enchantments.

Two times did not make a definitive pattern, but I was pretty sure some subtle magic made it impossible for me to discuss Ellie's situation with an elf.

I pulled out my phone. Time to test whether the inability to discuss concealment enchantment extended to werewolves. Mark

Ellis had acknowledged Ellie at Lara's Café, and Axlam already knew Ellie had a relationship with magic, so I had hope. I opened my messenger app fully intending to send a note to one of the Alfheim Pack's Alphas, Gerard Geroux, and ask a specific question.

My truck shook, and a hollow *bang* echoed through its frame.

I looked up from my phone and out the back window.

Benta the Nameless stood in the bed, her tight jeans low on her hips and the hem of her shirt high on her belly. Magic swirled off the enchantments tattooed around her waist—Benta was the only elf I had ever met who carried tracers and protection spells on her midriff. Body armor tended to cover and interfere with the magic, and as a whole, the elves were always battle-ready. Benta, though, had never seemed to be a fighter. A spy, perhaps, or a distraction. A lover, for sure. But never a woman who would carry an axe into a fight.

Benta was also not an elf who glamoured unless absolutely necessary, and even then only enough to cover her ears. She enjoyed the attention of mundanes, and minimal glamours held their attention. She often spent more of her time with the regular people of Alfheim then she did with her own kind.

The mundanes thought she was just Alfheim's tattooed-hipster animal-rescue expert who liked to wear her hair shaved on the sides and pulled back into a long, ice-black ponytail. Like all the elves, she watched the world through gray eyes, but hers had a fire to them that contrasted with the bluish tones of her hair.

She usually had on some type of cap to disguise her ears, and today she'd tied a scarf around her neck and wore a large, floppy, leather safari hat that shadowed her exquisitely beautiful, sharp features. She yanked on the hat and bent over to stare down at my toolbox.

Even through my truck's tinted rear window, her cleavage was just as gloriously distracting as I remembered it. She touched her lip and her breasts subtly squeezed together.

Benta hadn't changed at all since we were together.

I tucked away my phone. "What are you doing?" I called.

She looked up through the window, but did not straighten her back. "Well, hello, handsome," she purred.

Moments like this—with the feline-like purring and the suggestiveness—made me wonder if she should drop the Nameless and call herself Freyasdottir.

I scowled.

Benta laughed. "You *are* aging well, Frank. I swear with each passing decade you become less a dead thing and more the perfect male you were built to be."

I didn't know if I should be insulted or complimented. But that, too, was Benta.

"Get out of my truck," I said.

Benta stood tall and my view shifted from her cleavage to her waist. She wiggled her hips in a semi-consciously suggestive way, and tapped her foot. "You have Sal in your box." Her hand came into view and she touched the top of the toolbox.

"Sal?" The axe had a name? *Why didn't you tell me?* I thought.

A muffled mental shrug flowed out of the box.

"Oh!" Benta bounced on the balls of her feet. "Sal likes you!"

"*Sal* seems a bit pedestrian for an elven axe," I muttered.

The axe shrugged again.

Benta threw open the toolbox. "Since you are here, old friend, I do believe you should dance with us."

Sal seemed less than excited, but willing to cooperate. Benta picked her up.

Out of her glamour, Sal was as exquisite as Benta. The axe's foot-wide blade shimmered with silver and gold magic in the morning sun, with the runes glowing with liquid fire. Her handle gleamed as much from smoothness as from magic.

Sal was not a simple tool, nor was she meant for chopping wood.

The axe huffed. I got the distinct impression that she thought me shallow for focusing on her beauty and not her ability.

"You know better than that," Benta said to the axe. Then she grasped the wall of my truck's bed and vaulted over the side. She landed on the ground, axe on her shoulder, with a feline grace few elves other than Dag could match.

She adjusted Sal and her top as she walked toward the driver's side window, then pointed into the forest. "We broke up right over there."

We'd broken up before we had our final session of breaking up "right over there." Then I broke a tree.

I didn't stop drinking after Rose's death. Benta took pity on me anyway, even if she didn't like the alcohol. Yet part of me still wondered if she blamed me not only for Rose's out-of-control suicide, but also for the death of the elf who tried to help.

They'd been friends. Benta did not have a lot of elven friends, and my witch-daughter killed one of her closest.

I'd lost a daughter. Benta had lost an elf who'd been like a sister to her. We were drawn together by our mutual anguish, but the resulting sparks hadn't been the kind that started a long-lasting fire.

Then I snapped a tree in two and Benta walked away.

Sal seemed sadly amused by my relationship with the elf holding her handle.

Benta leaned against the door. "Dagrun says we have a vampire problem?" Benta, like all the elves, liked to switch topics. The conversation would likely come back to our break-up—Benta could—and likely was—holding every single word I said and every movement I made in her mind's eye. She played chess with the world, and figured out everyone's moves significantly farther ahead than they did.

It made her manipulative. It also made her uncannily observant and good at reading people.

"Yes," I said.

She nodded once. "Those two little insects, Tony and Ivan?" She glanced at me. "And something made by your father."

"Yes," I said again.

"Tony Biterson is significantly older than some Cold War spy," she said offhand. "Arne has always known."

I long ago guessed as much. "Ivan?" I asked.

Benta shrugged. "Ivan is an enigma."

"He appeared to me as a ghost," I said. "His human form. Nothing vampiric about him at all. He cleansed me of some sort of anger-inducing, slimy magic."

Benta's nose crinkled. "Odd."

I pulled the handle to exit the truck. "Quite." I swung out my feet. "I think Ivan's human half may be in revolt against his vampire."

Benta's eyebrow arched and she bit her lip. "Maybe." She stepped back to give me room and walked toward the trees.

I rounded the front of the truck. Right on the edge of the tree line sat a tawny cat about the size of a Shetland sheepdog. Gentle magic swirled across its fur in sweeping, calming patterns. The cat yawned, then ran its paw over its huge, tufted ear.

"Roxy, sweetie, come here," Benta said, and extended her hand to the cat. It stood, and like all cats, stretched first to show how little it cared about Benta's call, then padded over.

White and black rimmed Roxy's eyes, nose, and mouth. She looked like a jumper, with her sleek body and larger back legs.

"An African caracal?" I asked.

Roxy crouched. Her muscles coiled, and with one swift movement, she leaped from the ground to the top of my toolbox. She dropped down with her paws hanging off the side, and slow-blinked at Benta.

"I rescued her from a drug lord." She smiled. "He hand-raised her, so she's better with people than she ought to be. Isn't that right?"

Roxy ignored Benta.

"I was surprised we didn't find lions, tigers, and bears on that rescue." Benta looked up at me. "The mundanes who think it's macho to keep large carnivores tend to lack imagination."

"Does Gaupe know there's another cat in town?" Though I doubted Arne's lynx would care anymore than Roxy seemed to.

"They get along. Isn't that right?" Benta asked the cat.

Roxy continued to ignore us both.

Benta switched Sal to her other shoulder and pointed toward the trees. "I brought her because she's a good tracker."

Good thing I'd left Marcus Aurelius at... home. He wasn't with me, but I knew he was safe. He'd come home after being gone for a couple of days and I'd met... someone.

Benta touched my elbow. "Whoa... something shifted there, big guy."

I looked down at her.

"Not *you*. Something shifted against *me*."

Benta the Nameless pushed her floppy hat back on her head as she watched my face.

"I'm beginning to wonder if this is bigger than a few naughty vampires," she said, and turned toward the forest.

Naughty was not how I would describe my brother. *Evil* seemed most accurate. He hurt and he destroyed simply because he could. Tricksters were naughty. A trickster would set a trap and derive as much pleasure from watching a smart opponent foil a plan as from him falling victim. For tricksters, the goal was simply the game—not the ending.

For the evil, the game happened only to get their prey's blood pumping. The game was to make a tastier dinner.

I watched Roxy jump off my toolbox and pad into the trees. She was a cat. Cats played with their food, as did vampires. So why was my brother evil and not the caracal slinking through the underbrush?

Roxy wiggled her butt and pounced on a bug. Benta laughed and scratched the cat's head. Why was a cat's pouncing less evil than a vampire's?

Why was the thought of my brother in his dapper suit made of a witch's ashes so much more terrifying than any large predator?

Maybe because Victor Frankenstein's second son was the bigger, faster, smarter version of me—and I had an intimate understanding of the damage the rage of one of my father's sons could cause.

I followed Benta into the trees. A crow sounded an alarm—it must have noticed Roxy. Several other birds joined in, as did a squirrel or two. We trekked into the dappled early autumn sun, Benta and her cat in front, me following behind watching for threats.

"How quick was he?" Benta called. "Your brother?" She stopped and sniffed at a tree. "Is he as big and fast as you?"

Did my brother outrun the Alfheim Pack with a smoking wooden dagger in his shoulder? He'd seemed confused and diminished when he ran from the Carlson's burning house last night.

"Bigger," I said. "As for his speed, I don't know." I stopped a few feet back and watched Roxy stalk a snake slithering through a delicate bed of pink ladyslipper orchids. "Rose gave me a dagger," I said.

Something moved between Sal and Benta, who nodded as if listening.

Benta wasn't nearly as shocked at a century-dead witch giving me an artifact as I had expected. Often elves had a hard time believing such intricate and powerful magicks were possible.

Except Benta. But then again, Benta never seemed shocked by anything.

"It was about the length of your forearm," I continued. "And made of wood. Sharp as a metal blade, too. Sal and the dagger were incompatible magic, but they made some sort of 'enemy of my enemy' agreement, so I don't think it was bad magic."

Benta shifted Sal to her other shoulder as she turned toward me. "Not all dark magic is bad, and not all bad magic is dark," she said.

True, I thought. If adopting a witch had taught me anything, it was that magic was as complex in both nature and nurture as people. "It fell out of a blank spell book," I said.

Benta sniffed. "Do you still have the book?"

I thought for a moment. "I left it in the SUV Dag borrowed." I hadn't thought to ask Dag about it. "My brother rolled the vehicle." It was probably in the impound lot.

Sal agreed with my recollections.

"I need to call Ed," I said. Or Dag. Why did I forget about Rose's notebook? I pulled my phone out of my pocket.

I seemed to be forgetting a lot these days.

My phone had a new background photo. A beautiful red-haired woman hugging my dog.

"Her name is Ellie Jones," I said, and held up my phone for Benta to see. I should ask Benta something about Ellie. Something important. But I couldn't *remember*.

Benta shook as if a ghost had run a finger up her spine. "The shifting happened again, Frank." She turned away. "This *is* bigger than naughty vampires."

She wiggled her fingers suggestively. "Come here, son of Victor."

39

Elves skipped from topic to topic, but skipping from vampires to suggestiveness was outside of even Benta's normal behavior.

She frowned, then shook her head. "It's good to see you're still a man." She wiggled her fingers again. "But at this particular moment, Sal has more interest in your big, handsome body than I do, old friend."

The axe threw me what I could only read as a *I pick you*. Or more precisely, *You need me to pick you.*

Sal chose me over the elf.

Benta patted the axe but continued to frown. "One should never argue with magic."

I walked over. Benta looked up at me from under her floppy hat, her grey eyes dark and her face disappointed.

She held out Sal. "Take it."

I pinched the bridge of my nose. "I *can't*, Benta. You know that. Only an elf can touch an elven-made weapon."

She shrugged, and held the axe at chest height. She released Sal. Her hands did a swinging, circling move and her elbows squared to her body at the same time her magic lifted off her waist.

Sal did not fall. Every sigil, every enchantment and spell tattooed onto Benta's midriff lifted off her skin and formed a magical egg around the axe.

Gears formed. Energy pulleys aligned. Then the magical construction snapped in two.

Most of it returned to Benta's body. Some did not. Some became a new, blue-violet lacing weaving itself along Sal's handle. It criss-crossed itself into a herringbone basket pattern, and tightened down onto the wood.

Benta added a "glove" to the handle instead of my hands.

Sal hung in the air, supported by Benta's magic. "Go ahead," she said.

Energy crackled along the handle. This time, though, I felt the wood through the magic, so whatever Benta did was different from the gloves Dag had made the last time I touched the axe.

Sal didn't seem to care who held her, but did seem happier to be on my shoulder. "How long will the magic last?"

Benta shrugged again. "As long as you do well by the world."

I opened my mouth to ask all the necessary questions: What does that mean, specifically? Will I burn out the magic in a fight? Does Sal need special recharging?

The breeze changed direction and what had been a constant upwind wash over our backs flipped and became a momentary downwind push.

Benta squeezed my arm. "Do you smell that?"

"Yes." Meat and blood. Gore. A kill that likely happened overnight.

"Human," Benta breathed, and ran off through the trees with her caracal at her side.

I found her outside a dense thicket surrounded by two fallen and dying trees. The trunks interlocked and filled the area with a web of shadows and branches.

No person or animal was going to go digging in that mess.

I knew forests had "creepy" places—areas that held more death than life. They happened within any ecosystem when the balance of life and death tipped too much toward death. There was nothing extraordinarily magical about them, they just were.

This was one such spot, except this one smelled of human decay.

Roxy ran due west. Benta looked back at me and followed.

And there, around the base of one of the fallen trees, the cat found the body.

CHAPTER 6

We rounded the forest's creepy place and walked the thirty feet to the root ball. Benta untied her scarf and held it over her face. I didn't have the extra-sensitive nose of an elf, and though the stink made me gag, it wasn't bad enough I needed to cover my mouth.

Not yet.

The tree trunk had yanked up a good mound of soil when it tipped, and hid from sight what waited on the other side.

Flies buzzed. Roxy sniffed and trotted over to the roots, but she sidestepped the way frightened cats often sidestep, and her back arched. She hissed and darted back toward Benta.

The elf next to me put her hand on my arm. "The magic here. It's…" she shook her head. "I don't like it."

Nor did Roxy. I dropped Sal into my hands and moved to step forward, but Benta gripped my arm again. "Please don't go over there."

All I could see of her face was her jaw working as she stared at the tree from under her floppy leather hat.

"I need to check," I said.

Her magic flared. It burst outward from her body as patterned curtains of energy that bristled and stood up like the fur of a terrified cat.

"Benta?" I asked.

She continued to stare at the tree. "This is *not* just naughty vampires," she muttered.

"I think we're pretty clear on that," I said.

She tipped back her head enough I could see her eyes. The look she threw me brought back memories, none of them good. "Go on, then, son of Victor," she intoned.

I squared my shoulders and did my best not to groan. Benta knew how to push my buttons. At this point, I doubted she understood how she pushed any more than I understood what she was pushing. But civility was easily crushed between us and likely would always stay the fragile eggshell it was.

Sal threw me a distinctive *don't be pathetic* feel.

The axe understood more than it should. I made a mental note to make peace with the lovely—and distressed—elf standing at my elbow. If not for her, for me. And Sal.

"I trust your elf instincts," I said. "If they're telling you not to get close, then you need to stay back." I motioned toward the tree. "The last thing we need is one of Alfheim's strongest elves attacked by a demonic, vampiric magic we don't understand."

Benta opened her mouth, then closed it and bit her lip.

I knew exactly what she was thinking—she saw her own refusal to move in as a sign of weakness.

I handed her Sal. "There is *unknown* magic here, Benta," I said. "I would feel better if you listened to your gut and observed."

I walked toward the upturned base of the tree before she could argue.

The stink hit me full in the face as I rounded the dirt and tangled roots.

What remained of a man's body sat in a hollow deep inside the ball, hunched over and wrapped in the roots and dead grasses very much like a meal cocooned by a spider.

My brother, in his manipulations before his outright attacks, had thralled two men. They did his daylight dirty business, and had been responsible for the video that caught Maura and Akeyla out of their glamour—the video which had almost gotten my adoptive sister and niece banished to Hawaii. Brother murdered one and left him on the Carlson's lakeshore the night before the house burned. The other one had vanished.

Or so we thought.

Not much was left of him. He'd been chewed up, and from the lack of blood in the area, drained dry. But the flies still buzzed and the flesh still rotted—and rotted more than it should have in the little time feasible for him to be encased in the tree.

I looked around the roots. "Benta?" I yelled. "Can creepy places like the one this tree borders accelerate decay?"

She held Sal like a shield. "Yes," she said.

At her side, Roxy growled at the now fully-rancid air. Benta responded with her own low, guttural snarl. A new wave of stink made me gag and I covered my nose with the back of my hand.

I knew enough about police work to stay back. I could disturb the one clue Ed—or in this case, Arne—needed. I glanced at Benta. She recoiled every time the breeze blew a new whiff of death toward us. She wouldn't come near the tree.

Which made me wonder if all the elves would react the same way.

"How did the pack miss this?" Benta shouted. "How did we?"

The man would have been difficult to see at night. The wolves, though, could scent out a roadkill squirrel half-a-mile away.

I knelt where I was and peered between the roots. The sun had hit high enough in the sky that a shaft of light had pierced the gloom and hit the gnawed-up remains of the man's shoulder.

A dark, slimy magic oozed toward the light, then sprang back like a shocked snake.

"There's dark magic." I said. "The sun is puncturing it." The new hole was letting out the decay.

"Frank," Benta called. "This slimy magic you spoke of, did you get a sense of *animal* from it?"

"This magic, here in the tree, yes," I said. "It's darker than what

Ivan cleansed from me."

"And more... alive?" she asked.

Maybe. I stood. "In none of my interactions with my brother was I able to see his magic. I perceived only the forms he made of the ash he stole from Rose's Hill." But even from my current place a good seven or more feet from the body, I could still see the dark magic oozing over the corpse. "Except when Ivan's ghost made it visible."

"Did you happen to tell Arne or Dag that the magic with which your brother infected you felt *alive*?"

"No." I backed away from the tree. "Honestly, it didn't occur to me." None of this "living magic" business occurred to me until Sal made it blindingly obvious that it could occur. Magic mostly operated in a sort of mechanical way—like the gearwork spells of Dag's magical armor, or the natural geometry of the sigils around Benta. How could something so clock-like be "alive" alive? Yet Sal sure seemed to be a thinking being.

So really, the oily magic of my brother's infection hadn't felt alive. Just sticky.

But then again, slime molds were alive.

"What are we dealing with here, Benta?" I asked.

She stepped back, as well. "And your brother moved in and out of The Land of the Dead?"

"Yes," I said. Lots of magical creatures could move in and out of the different realms.

"Roxy!" Benta called. "Come!" She slapped her leg as if calling a dog, not a cat. "I *knew* it," Benta said. "We're dealing with low-demons."

I had been infected with a *demon*?

I set Sal against my leg and pulled out my phone. Arne and Dag needed to know about this.

The picture. The woman. Ellie Jones. I looked up at Benta, then back at the phone. "Benta?" I said. Nothing else would come out of my mouth.

"What?" She took a step toward me.

And I forgot the woman's name.

"Stop!" I raised my hand. "Step back. Please."

Benta backed up.

"Her name is Ellie," I said. A shiver rattled my spine and tightened my belly. I needed to pay attention.

I *had* to pay attention… I dropped my phone into the leaf litter under my feet.

A shadow moved over not only me, but also Benta and Roxy on the other side of the tree.

The dark, oily magic had risen up out of the tree while I was distracted by the picture on my phone. It sprang from the roots like a thirty-foot cobra with its hood spread wide. If it had been physical, it would have blocked the sun.

It shuddered as if shrieking. Rage boiled off it in the sun, its oily parts shaking and locking in the light, but it would not be deterred. It wanted. It *needed*. It had to be fed.

And like any predator, it had snuck up on its prey while I was preoccupied.

Sal screamed. This magic was not the 'enemy of my enemy' magic with which she'd made a deal to help stop my brother. The magic gurgling off the root ball was truly black—and like her, conscious.

Not conscious as in writing poems and plays, but conscious like Roxy, or the squirrels in the trees, but not quite Marcus Aurelius. The black magic around the body was responsive enough that it adapted to the environment. It had needs and it would slither around until it sated its drives. We weren't dealing with a spell, or an enchantment.

An unconcealed low-demon.

Benta shouted again for Roxy to come, but the cat didn't sense magic the way we did. She didn't react fast enough. She didn't know what to do.

The magic of the dark thing burned up in the sun, but it attacked anyway. And just before it turned fully to broken, dusted bits, it descended onto Roxy.

The cat screamed. Nothing physical had her; nothing she could smell or bite. But the slimy underbelly of magic, the writhing rage-oil that pools in the darkest parts of The Lands, landed on her feline soul.

I gripped Sal. The energy bands lifted up and tied my hand to her handle and I got the impression that Sal did not want me to put her down.

"All right, then," I said, and swung at the low-demon.

It sprang back and hissed out a stream of ash.

Real ash. Dark, thick, oily ash like the remains of Rose's cottage. The ash my brother stole. Ash it spit like venom into my eyes and nose.

I coughed. Sal groaned. I stumbled and wiped at my face.

"Roxy!" Benta screamed.

Where was the cat? Ten feet to my left, out of grabbing distance, and too close to the low-demon. I twisted around, then back toward Benta as she ran toward her cat.

I snagged the elf around her waist.

"Don't touch Roxy!" Benta screamed at the low-demon. She couldn't see the magic. She saw only her beast's agony. But I knew that even though the magic diminished in the sun, it still slithered. It still raged.

Sal wanted to slash. Sal wanted to cut the low-demon, but I *knew*, somehow, that I needed to keep both the axe and the elf back. Because Benta couldn't see the magic, it would slither around her defenses. I'd lose not only her cat, but Benta herself.

Roxy howled. She snarled and her back hunched. And she changed.

What had been a sleek and beautiful caracal turned black and hideous. Her eyes clouded, then crystalized, then turned to red embers. Her fur darkened. Ash puffed off her coat.

"Let go of me!" Benta screamed. She flipped out her hands and drew up her magic.

"No! Benta!" I stepped between her and her now-possessed caracal. "No tracers. No enchantments. That's what it wants." It would use the enchantment to get to her. "My brother used my tracers! He turned the glamour around The Great Hall to his advantage! You can't feed it."

Roxy hissed. Her tail flicked. Demonic flame danced across the tufts on her ears. She darted under the fallen tree, out of view, out of the sun, and deep into the forest's death-creepy place.

She wouldn't come out again until the sunset.

"Roxy!" Benta panted. She hit my chest. "You goddamned monster! You let this happen."

"How is this *my* fault?" I roared. Why, with Benta, was everything my fault?

She hit me again. "You see magic! You didn't know what it was?" Her sigils lifted off her midriff. They swirled in the air and pulled in her other magic. Benta bristled.

Maybe I should have let her intervene. Maybe she could have cleaned out whatever took Roxy. But my gut said no.

I'd spent last week with what had probably been a rage-magic low-demon coating me and altering my behavior. I engaged in stupid and reckless behaviors—I tossed a tracer enchantment into The Land of the Dead. I sent my high-demonic brother the light he needed to find the path into Alfheim.

I had no idea how long I'd carried the low-demon. When had my brother sent it? How had it gotten past the elves' defenses?

But low-demons hide. They're like rats—they could be under the floorboards and you might never know.

Yet someone attached one to me. That kind of spellwork could only be handled by someone with knowledge—and someone who was here long before my brother appeared.

Ivan. It had to be Ivan.

"I'm beginning to think the Bitersons were biding time," I said.

Benta hit my arm. "Arne and his damned need to be modern! I told him allowing those two in was a mistake! But no, he thought he could tame them. Rehabilitate, he said. He thought they were like the pack. They're demons!"

Demons who turned Alfheim's magicks against her residents.

The tracers I carry on my arms are small spells. Tiny, compared to the magic Benta was capable of releasing. What if that thing had twisted her up into a death-shadow the way it twisted Roxy?

"Benta, I'm sorry."

She wailed and hit me again. "I *will* trap it," she snarled. "I *will* free my cat." She pulled away. "Go away."

Benta pushed me toward the truck. She picked up Sal and waved her at me. "Go away!" Benta screamed.

I needed to call this in. Ed needed to know about the body, and Arne and Dag about Roxy.

I looked around for my phone. The sun hit the screen and a glint popped between the leaves. I scooped it up and shoved it into my pocket. I'd call once I had Benta away from here.

"Let's go," I said.

Her fingers tensed. She held Sal like a talisman and raised her arms in a strong, dancer-like way.

Benta the Nameless was about to cast an enchantment on me.

I scooped her up and threw her over my shoulder. She tried to smack me with Sal's handle but thankfully, the axe would have none of that.

"I told you a century ago that if you ever again tried to enchant me against my will I would tie you to a tree and leave you in the woods for a week."

She slapped my back. "You said no such thing! You damned brute!"

My actual words had been something coarse about her magic no longer being welcome. And then I broke a tree in two.

I carried Benta toward the truck. "We have no idea at all what we are dealing with here," I said. "Have you ever seen a low-demon turn an animal vampire?"

She inhaled sharply. "No."

I stopped trudging through the trees and dropped her to her feet. "Please don't run off," I said. "And please don't go off half-cocked with the magic, okay? That's what started all this."

Benta held out Sal. "Take her."

I placed the axe on my shoulder.

Benta adjusted her top, then her floppy hat. She closed her eyes, but didn't speak. Then Benta the Nameless, one of Alfheim's most powerful elves, turned her back to me and walked toward my truck.

49

CHAPTER 7

I called Arne as I followed Benta out of the woods. "He's escalated," I said, and hung up. Best to speak of dead bodies in person.

I'd been correct in front of Lara's. Finding the Bitersons was a priority, but finding my brother—walking and talking, as a pile of sun-made dust, or as the dead corpse he should be, it didn't matter —*had* to happen. We needed to know one way or the other if and how the vampires were using the low-demons.

I called Ed and left a message. He was probably still asleep.

Benta said nothing on the walk back to the truck. Slowly, with each step away from the place where the low-demon had taken her cat, her magic contracted around her body.

Benta's magic formed up into long, wavering sigils that looked more like tiger stripes than the gearwork I was used to seeing.

She'd left her vehicle in a patch of sunlight just off the dirt tracks leading to Rose's Hill. She stood at the taillight of her "Alfheim Wildcat Sanctuary" SUV inside a cat-like magic armor not all that different from the one Dag's magic had built right after my brother first appeared.

Never in my life had I seen Benta respond to the world in such a flat, controlled way. She made no expression. She walked with a deceptive ease.

She pulled her keys out of her pocket. "I will confer with Dag and Arne." Her tone said I was not welcome at the meeting.

"Fine," I said. "Do not bend what happened into my fault, Benta."

She scowled. "Go home."

Benta got into her SUV and drove down the dirt track and back toward town, most likely on her way to speak with Alfheim's royal family.

The last flash from Benta's brake lights reflected through the trees' shadows and the hum of her engine vanished. I was alone with only Sal and my thoughts.

Behind me, up the side of a steep hill, sat the ruins of Rose's cottage. Ahead of me, my own truck, the dirt tracks, and either town or my own home. I rubbed my face. I should go in. Find Rose's notebook. Find Ed. State my case with Arne. Help organize tonight's defense against... what? A vampire attack? The return of my weakened brother? Demons? Evil possessed cats? I had no idea.

Dark magic sowed dark chaos.

Which, honestly, was the heart of the issue here. Dark magic fertilized evil soil and now all sorts of problems wiggled from spores left in the darkest shadows.

This was the way of the horror of the world. It moved as a rolling bank of mist out of which all sorts of terrors manifested.

Never one. Never a singular threat. Always a swarm. There might be one huge problem—vampires, in this case—but that problem was always a swarm of smaller, individual issues.

Issues such as Ivan and who—or what—he really was. Or if he truly was a low-demon Pied Piper. Or Tony's true identity. Or if my brother was still around.

Or, if in his diminished state, he was still my "brother."

I looked up at Rose's Hill.

I was wrong. Evil wasn't a predator. Evil was a stampeding swarm of rats that would as soon trample you into the ground as suck you dry.

I closed my eyes and inhaled. I needed to stay calm and clear-headed. Nothing fed evil faster than undifferentiated fear.

But why did I feel I had—

Ellie.

I slapped my truck's fender. Something about the concealment enchantments hiding Ellie made it impossible for me to ask the elves for help—or to have them comprehend that I was asking for help.

When Benta and I were in the woods, I'd pulled out my phone not once, but *twice*. And both times I'd spoken Ellie's name.

Neither time registered with Benta—or Sal. If Benta had noticed, she would have asked. Benta liked to know about the people in town. She might not like dealing with most of them, but she liked understanding who and what they were.

So Ellie's name had floated right by Benta and the bright, elven magic enchanting my axe.

"Do you know anything about fae concealments?" I asked Sal.

The axe did not respond.

I hopped up into the bed of my truck and flipped open the toolbox. "You tired?" I asked.

Still no response.

I flicked a hammer to the side and made room for Sal. "Take a nap. Think about what just happened," I said. "Focus on the low-demon." Maybe the enchanted axe would come up with a low-demon battle plan while snuggling with my tape measure.

Again, no response.

I closed the toolbox. I was fighting two very different wars on two fronts and my gut told me that the magicks involved were interfering with each other in some areas, and amplifying each other in others.

Right now, Sal sure felt interfered-with.

I glanced up at Rose's Hill. She used to write spells, draw symbols, and tack stories and images onto the walls of her cottage, and then copy down her thoughts into notebooks.

Maybe Rose wasn't as crazy as we all thought. Maybe she was on to something.

I backed my truck around and made my way toward Alfheim's Impound Lot.

Time to delineate the issues and sort this mess.

ALFHEIM'S Impound Lot was a fenced-off section sublet from Gullinbursti—"We recycle so you don't have to!"—Reclamations. Gullinbursti's main office was a square little building situated in a square little parking lot under a sign of a big, bristling, golden hog. To the left of the building, a gate leading into the leased Impound. To the right, a second gate leading into the main junkyard.

Dag's main reason for the city subletting from Gullinbursti was that around here, impounded vehicles either ended up junked or resold, so why not dump them into the local car resale business from the get-go?

Like so much of the town, Gullinbursti was owned by Magnus Freyrsson.

Pretty much everyone loved Magnus. He exuded a lovable magic, but mostly he was well-mannered, handsome, and charismatic. However, Magnus came with his own set of issues.

He'd once been a movie star. Before talkies, he'd made a minor name for himself as the handsome actor who never removed his hat while on set, or on camera. He managed his glamours well, and never once got caught with his ears out.

Thing was, with Magnus, the elves were much more concerned about him whipping out other parts for the world to see. Seemed Magnus Freyrsson took his fertility god namesake a little too seriously, especially now that he had a phone with a camera and perpetual access to the internet.

So Magnus was one of the "managed" elves who, if left to their own devices, would get either themselves—or all the elves—into a whole lot of trouble.

Magnus always had an entourage. Always. Magnus alone for a day meant Alfheim would have a new adoration cult on its hands before the sunset. Magnus wasn't even allowed to go fishing by himself.

Still, Magnus was excruciatingly likeable. Arne and Dag often brought him along to important meetings, as long as he promised to *not* literally charm the pants off anyone.

In the two hundred years I've lived with the elves, not once had I seen him complain. He loved the attention, and so the elves fed his attentive needs while keeping him modernly under control.

Gullinbursti's door chimed as I walked in. Today, Magnus's handler turned out to be Mark Ellis, the newbie wolf who'd been at Lara's this morning.

Mark sat at a desk behind the counter in the front room of the main building. The room hadn't been redecorated in decades and had moved from ugly, to dated, to "quaintly retro" with its burnt-orange vinyl waiting room seating, dark-but-real wood paneling, and a big honest-to-the-gods old-school console television.

Actual living lavender freshened the air. No elf or wolf was going to work all day in a space scented by chemicals, so even if the interior was ugly, it smelled nice.

Mark looked up and smiled. "Frank!" He stood and walked to the counter. "Need a part?"

Like a lot of the male wolves, Mark Ellis wasn't particularly big. There seemed to be a physical type that made it through a bite alive— medium build, strong but not bulky, shorter than the elves but not too short, and fast. They were, as Remy liked to say, good Special Ops recruits.

The last time I was military, we were fighting other Americans about human rights. But I did understand the type. The nondescript guys who didn't stand out and who could wiggle in and out of any situation. Mark even had brown hair and blue eyes like eighty percent of the local mundanes.

He'd changed into his blue-gray Community Service Officer uniform since I saw him this morning, and a police belt, though he wasn't carrying.

"No parts today, Mark," I said. Gullinbursti's sold a lot of used truck and car parts, plus parts for three-wheelers, jet skis, boats, and radiators. You name it, Gullinbursti's could get it for you.

"Mr. Freyrsson is in the back." Mark nodded toward the computer. "He's talking to one of the Maori contacts in New Zealand." He leaned closer. "A fertility spirit. She's consoling him about his horses." He shook his head. "Last I heard they were still missing four or five. I'll be taking Mr. Freyrsson out to the stables when he's done here."

I hoped we were only dealing with frightened horses, but now I wondered. Still, I didn't want to get into that conversation with Mark.

He pointed over his shoulder. "Mr. Freyrsson says he has more privacy to talk here instead of up at the dealership." He chuckled. "They're emotionally supporting each other."

I chuckled, too. "Magnus can be a handful."

Mark rolled his eyes. "I think he's in love."

In love. Ellie. I'd almost forgotten again.

"Mark," I said, and pulled out my phone. "Do you remember this woman?"

Mark frowned. "Should I?"

He'd acknowledged Ellie at the Café, but didn't remember her now. The concealment enchantments affected the wolves, too, but not as much as the elves. But then again, the wolves, at least in human form, were less magical.

The enchantments must be calibrated to the power level of the magical in question.

Mark pointed at my phone. "Is she one of Mr. Freyrsson's conquests?"

I'll snap his elf neck if he messes with her, I thought, then realized what I was thinking. Had that low-demon infected me with rage again? Except I didn't feel rage. Protectiveness, yes. A bit of possessiveness. Attraction, for sure. But not rage.

Mark seemed to read my expression. He laughed. "Keep her away from him, buddy," he said.

I tucked away my phone. "Magnus came over with Arne," I said. "He's old and thinks he's entitled to his ways." Modern mundanes no longer agreed, hence the minding, but part of me was relieved he wouldn't notice Ellie. Not with her concealments. It was one less thing I needed to worry about.

Mark shrugged and changed the subject. "What brings you out here?"

"I need into the Impound Lot," I said.

"Do you have the paperwork?" Of course Mark would keep it official. If he screwed up his job, there'd be no further officer training for him.

"Could you call Ed?" I asked. "Or Dag? She borrowed the SUV I rolled last night. I left something in it I need to get." I pointed toward the lot outside. "I don't know who owns the vehicle."

The backroom door swung open. Magnus Freyrsson crossed his arms, leaned against the jamb, and smiled one of his disarming smiles.

He wore a crisp, white, well-tailored button down complete with silver cufflinks, and an expensive leather belt with a matching silver buckle. Magic coiled out from around the collar like a cartoon version of the expensive French cologne Magnus must be wearing.

Magnus dropped his hundred-dollar-haircut glamour, though his clothes continued to be the immaculate and crisp shirt and slacks. His eyes changed from the arresting blue-green that matched much of his magic to their natural, elven gray. The also-natural pattern of naked scalp above the ears manifested, as did his well-trimmed and tamed lynx-like sideburns and well-groomed beard.

All male elves had cat-like sideburns. Most shaved their beards. Magnus preferred to keep his at itchy length—not so long it needed combing, but longer than a five o'clock shadow. It highlighted his naturally square jaw in a way that I had to admit looked good. Even among the elves, Magnus was an outlier in the good looks department.

"The SUV's mine," Magnus said. "I allowed our beautiful Queen to borrow it because I knew she needed to transport her favorite son." He pointed at me and winked.

He might be extraordinarily likable, but on occasion his beauty and charm wore thin, which was yet another reason he and I did not socialize. Magnus was to Arne what Charles Brandon had been to

Henry VIII—buddy, confidante, and the wealthy, entertaining Lord who kept the court in running order when the King needed a break.

Or maybe he was more a college buddy. They were two of the few remaining original elves.

Magnus adjusted his cuffs. "Come." He pulled a set of keys off a pegboard and walked toward the counter. "I'll take you out to the car."

Mark shrugged. "He owns it, so there's no issue," he said.

"Thanks." I tapped the counter.

Mark returned to his desk as Magnus glamoured and stepped around the counter. He smiled yet again, and winked once more. "So you were out with our lovely Nameless One while my horses run wild, huh?"

I frowned. "Dag tell you that?"

Magnus opened the side door leading out into the Impound Lot. "Benta clings to you, my friend." He inhaled as if smelling the best of a spring day.

But he stopped. Confusion danced across his brow. "Dag, Maura, our adorable fire elf, and a... mostly-mundane." He shook it off and motioned for me to exit into the Lot. "You are a busy man, Mr. Victorsson."

"I just need to check the SUV, Magnus. That's all." Though "a mostly-mundane" meant something. What, I could not remember.

Magnus didn't seem to care, or at least had moved on from the thought.

He tossed me the SUV keys. "She's pretty banged up," he said. "The axles are good, as is the drive system. Engine checked out. They drove her here from where she rolled, which is damned good, considering. I'll have the guys bang out the side panels, fix the alignment, and tune her up, and she'll be salable."

I was surprised both axles hadn't snapped. The SUV sat in the center of the lot, scratched and dented, but on its own tires. "I'm impressed," I said, and hit the key fob.

She beeped as I walked around to the back, and the doors unlocked.

Magnus patted the SUV. "You want her? I'll give you a good price."

I had my truck. "It's just me," I said, though something nipped at the side of my mind. It might be nice for "just me" to have a second vehicle available. I couldn't remember why. "I'll think about it," I said. Seemed the best answer.

Magnus sniffed at the air. "A shift, Mr. Victorsson," he said. "In the magic." Then he shook as if resetting and smiled at me once again.

I popped open the back of the SUV.

Rose's notebook had wedged itself into the space between the back seats and the cargo area. I crawled in and pulled it out.

He sniffed again. "*That* was in the back of my SUV?"

Magnus's glamour shimmered. For a split second, his elven emotions seeped through. Alfheim's most handsome elf almost showed the world an ugly incredulity.

"Yes." Why was he surprised by this? He'd been in the building next to the lot all morning. "Is this the first time you've checked the vehicle since it was brought in?" Perhaps he hadn't realized.

His eyes narrowed. "Witch magic," he grumbled.

I took that as a *yes*. "I'll take it with me," I said. He wouldn't have to deal with the notebook at all.

"Keep the keys." He turned around. "Get that witch-touched vehicle off my lot, Mr. Victorsson," he said, and walked away.

I watched him go. What else could I do? I pocketed the keys and patted the side of the SUV. "I guess you're mine now." I didn't know what I would do with a beat-up, though fully-loaded, SUV. She was drivable, at least. Maybe Magnus would give me a deal on bodywork, as long as I promised only to have mundanes work on her.

This, like the evil swarm of vampire issues, was a moment of magical complexity. Waves of magic flowed in from different directions and some crests added to each other. Some troughs subtracted. But nothing was canceled. Nothing made a smooth, magic-free moment.

Of course not, I thought. Why would I catch a break? Like Benta said, not all light magic was good.

My phone rang.

"Dag," I said, as I answered.

"Low-demons," she said.

"Looks like it."

Dag paused. "And the dark rage that attached to you was one?"

Benta must have given Dag a detailed accounting. Hopefully, she didn't lay all the blame at my feet. "Benta seems to think so."

"Tell Magnus to come in." She paused again. "And go home. Rest, Frank. Let us deal with this."

"Coming in" meant a call was about to go out to all the elves in Alfheim. Everyone was to meet at The Great Hall—and the powerful elves were looking for a quorum.

No one other than the elves would be allowed in. Not me. Not the wolves. Only Alfheim's Nordic magicals.

The Norse called it a Thing. They gathered for governance, trade and talk, and for the hashing out of disagreements.

And to deal with a town infestation.

"Are you sure about that, Dag?" I asked. "My brother is just as much my problem as he is the elves'." Not that I understood how to handle low-demons.

Dag paused. "You do not carry the sins of your father, Frank Victorsson."

But I was the son of Victor, as was my brother. "I can handle him, Dag." I lied. I knew deep in my bones that I could not handle my father's other son without the magic of the elves, but that did not mean I wouldn't try.

I had to try. Not trying would put all of Alfheim at risk.

"Let magic deal with magic," she said.

They'd called a Thing after Rose imploded. They organized and re-established the town's magical defenses then, too.

"Let us cleanse the town of this darkness," she said. "Then you can go after the monster your father inflicted on this Earth. But I will not allow my adopted son to go into a fight half-cocked. We're dealing with smart vampires. First, we diminish their power. Then we cut off their heads."

Like any good queen, Dag wanted to protect her people, including me.

"Besides, you need to sleep. I am not the only citizen of Alfheim in need of recuperation."

She had a point. "I'll go home," I said. If the elves took care of the dark magicks, it might also make finding the Bitersons and my brother easier. They would stick out more in the newly-brightened environment, so to speak.

"Thank you, Frank," Dag said.

"I'll rest."

She hung up. I looked down at my phone's screen. Ellie smiled up at me.

A wave was crashing into a rolling cloud of evil and I was standing right at the contact point.

The elves of Alfheim were about to organize and re-establish the town's magical defenses.

They were about to set off a wave-and-mist-clearing nuclear bomb. No demon—high or low—could stand against it.

"Magnus!" I called as I walked toward the building. He might be mad about witch magic on his SUV but he'd listen to Dag.

He stepped out the door and leaned against the jamb in much the same way he had the other door. "Yes?" He smiled a deceptively congenial smile and pointed into the shop. "Mark and I are heading out to the stables to find my missing horses."

"I'm sure they're fine," I said. "Your horses are smart."

He grinned. "You are always welcome to ride, Mr. Victorsson."

Magnus, for all his bombastic likeability, really was a generous elf. "Thank you." I held up my phone. "Dag called. She wants you to come in."

His expression immediately shifted from congenial to serious. "Because of the dark magic?"

"And the low-demons," I said.

He gripped my shoulder. "Go home." He looked out toward greater Alfheim. "Someone will call you in the morning."

They needed a day, at least, to organize, then the swarm of issues would cease to be a swarm—because after their magic exploded, no issues would be left to crawl out of any mist, good or bad.

Magnus pointed at the notebook. "Now, please remove that thing from my property."

I shook my head.

Magnus winked yet again and walked back into the building.

The elves would deal with the low-demons and their slithering dark magic.

Ellie, I thought. How would this affect her?

I tucked the notebook under my arm. I'd leave the SUV's keys with Mark and ask to have someone drop it off at my place.

Then I made my way to my truck.

CHAPTER 8

M arcus Aurelius bounded around my house, his tail wagging
and his head high. He barked a greeting before turning in a
circle.

I stood at my tree-side front door, the notebook in one hand and
my house key in the other, with the mid-afternoon sun on my back
and my dog trying very hard to get me to follow him instead of going
inside.

"All right, boy. All right." I tucked my keys back into my pocket and
followed him through my twisted and broken wine bottle gate.

Arne and my brother had fought outside my house just before
Brother attacked Akeyla at the Carlson house. Not only was my gate
broken, but most of my outdoor lighting had been stripped out.
They'd ripped off one of my deck rails. I also had a hole in my siding
where Brother had slammed Arne against the house.

The house had no broken windows, but Arne's blood still stained
my deck, and my elf-gifted, one-of-a-kind artsy gate needed repairs.

I should have asked Mark Ellis about new hinges while I was at
Gullinbursti's. I folded the gate so it leaned against the fence.
Maybe if—

My phone rang. I pulled it out and looked at the incoming number, which I did not recognize.

The number was listed as me. "Frank Victorsson" it said. I answered. "Hello?"

"Marcus Aurelius is happy you're home," a woman said—and not just from my phone. The most beautiful woman I had ever seen in my life stepped around the back corner of my house and onto the walk. She wasn't elven beautiful. No one but the elves was their kind of beautiful. This woman, with her reddish hair, big eyes, and perfect curves, was human beautiful.

She watched me notice her, and she tipped her head slightly to the side. Her mouth opened a little bit, and a small, embarrassed smile flitted across her lips. Then she disconnected the call.

"I thought I'd test the number." She tucked the phone into the pocket of her jeans. "I tried from my cottage but the call wouldn't go through. I think it's the enchantments."

She lived behind a wall of concealment enchantments.

Ellie, I thought. *Ellie Jones.* We met this morning.

The morning flooded back. The phone, and the food truck. Mark Ellis noticing her, then not remembering—and how being around elves blocked my memories. "Ellie?" I said. "I forgot that you'd be here."

I covered the distance between us before the last word was out of my mouth, and pulled her close for a hug.

I didn't ask. I don't know why. I'm careful about touching others, partly because the elves have rules, and partly because I'm bigger than everyone around me. I know I'm frightening. And I'm not exactly can-get-away-with-anything Magnus Freyrsson handsome.

But I had to touch her. I needed to know that she wasn't a mirage. "I'm sorry I forgot," I said.

She didn't pull away. She didn't stiffen. She sank into my embrace as if I was the one person in the world she trusted to protect her from the storms.

I breathed in the fresh, lavender scent of her hair. I felt her warmth, and the beat of her heart.

I needed to remember her. I *had* to.

She touched my chest and slowly pulled away. "There's no getting around the forgetting." But she smiled up at me anyway.

I looked around the corner at my deck. My backpack—the backpack I filled for her this morning—sat on one of the benches next to a paperback novel and a half-consumed bottle of water. She'd flung her hoodie over the back of one of the deck chairs. A wooden box with what looked like a lens attachment rested in a shady spot, and a smaller leather satchel sat on the chair's cushion. "How long have you been waiting?"

She stuck her hands into her back pockets, and her breasts thrust out. "Not long." She smiled again. "My leg feels better and it's nice to be outside."

She'd bruised her leg badly enough that she'd been limping this morning. I glanced down at her thigh. She did look as if she was carrying her weight more evenly. "How fast do you heal?" Sometimes magical people healed faster, but not always.

She shrugged. "I don't know." Her face tightened up the way it had this morning when she said she thought the enchantments edited her life. "But this bruise is healing a lot faster than it should." She looked down at her leg. "Maybe it's because I landed in a magical place?"

"Seems as possible an explanation as any I have." I offered my arm anyway, as we walked onto the deck. I needed to talk to her about the elves resetting Alfheim's magic, but first we should get settled.

"I brought a book from my library," she said. "I also took a photo of the Carlson house." She first pointed at the wood box, then at the ruins across the lake. "I'll develop it tonight."

She placed her hand on my forearm and her fingers curled around my skin.

Ellie touched one of my tracer enchantments.

The tracers were a gift from Dag. The tracers were to give me options in situations where I could not—or should not—follow a person or creature that might do me great harm. The tracers allowed the elves to track, and to deal with, threats. The tracers were, in many ways, magical GPS tags.

I don't use them much. I don't need to. I'm big and frightening, and more often than not, I take care of problems on my own.

My brother manipulated me into giving him one of the tracers so that he could track in reverse and find his way out of The Land of the Dead—the first time in one hundred years of carrying the tracers that they had not served me well.

And now Ellie recoiled as if she'd just been bitten by a snake.

"Ow!" she yelled, and shook her hand. "That *stung*." She danced around, still howling, and sucked on her finger.

I stood there, dumbfounded, wondering if Ellie was about to run away and leave me here all alone with my dog and my beat-up house.

She stopped dancing and shaking her hand when she looked up at my face.

"Are you okay?" I asked. Should I check her hand? Dare I touch her again? What if she did run off?

Her mouth rounded again and her eyes widened once more. She held out her hand. "I don't think there's damage," she said. "No blisters."

"I'm sorry." I peered at her hand. "I didn't realize the tracers would react that way to your enchantments." We could touch, just not bare skin on certain parts of my arms.

"Do I need to be careful of all your tattoos?" Her voice held only a hint of suggestiveness. The question was real and sincere but damn it, the magic on my body was not the magic occupying my mind.

"I don't know." But I wouldn't touch again unless invited. I wouldn't do anything to scare her in any way. Or cause her pain. Providing an anchor into the world from which the concealment enchantments hid her was my priority with Ellie.

She reached for my hand. Carefully, she rolled my arm over and looked at the visible tattoos of my tracers.

The enchantments themselves floated just above my skin and were probably what shocked her, not the actual elven silver ink. She stepped closer and reached toward my head.

I flinched. I didn't mean to, I just didn't want her to suffer another shock.

"Sorry," she said. "I'd like to know."

I braced myself.

Ellie touched my cheek. She touched and for a second I couldn't breathe. Not from any magic, but because as she glided her fingers over my skin, she moved toward the protection tattoos on my scalp.

Carefully, she touched my Yggdrasil tattoo.

Nothing happened. I exhaled.

But she pulled her hand away from the protection spells. "My fingers are tingling." She stuck her hands in her pockets again. "What do you think?"

I touched my scalp. "The Yggdrasil tattoo is also magical. Not protection or tracer, but a marker." It marks me as protected by the Alfheim elves.

"Maybe it's spells that might interfere with my enchantments?"

"Maybe," I said. Part of me hoped it was that simple, but another part shook its head and reminded me that nothing—absolutely nothing—about today's magical events was simple.

Still, I could hope.

"Tell you what," Ellie said, "let's go in and I'll show you what I found in my library." She patted Marcus Aurelius's head. "Besides, I think the emperor is tired and wants a nap."

My dog barked.

I walked up the deck toward the house to unlock my wide French doors. Maybe I should give her my extra key. I probably shouldn't. We just met. And I was paying for her phone. She'd been skittish about that. A key would probably send her running away permanently.

I unlocked the door.

I glanced back at Ellie. I'd been over-protective with Benta. Overzealous, she used to say. When we broke up, she called me "the world's biggest puppy." I, Frank Victorsson, the lumbering patchwork man who scared the living daylights out of most mundanes, "over-compensated."

I obviously still wore my heart on my sleeve.

Benta could be downright mean. Though I suppose "puppy" is better than "monster" any day.

But I needed to be careful. I needed to be the man Dag thought me to be.

I waved Ellie over. "Are you hungry?" I had no idea how well the cottage of hers fed her, even though she'd told me this morning that she didn't need groceries. Even if I was a puppy, I could at least be a puppy who made a good meal.

"Yes!" Ellie said, and stuffed her book into the backpack.

CHAPTER 9

I set Rose's notebook on the table. It hadn't done anything or
shown any indication of magic since I pulled it out of the SUV. It
just... sat there, like any old book. Nor did Ellie pay any attention
to it.

She walked by and set the backpack on the stool next to the
kitchen counter. She set the leather satchel on the granite, and pulled
out the wooden box I'd noticed outside.

"Your house is beautiful," she said. "The light, the space—they're
perfect." The French doors opened into the kitchen, which opened
into a dining-den area. My living room sat off to the side, and a
hallway led toward the three bedrooms, the bath, the stairs up to the
loft, and the foyer for the front door.

I'd planned it myself, and built the entire house scaled to my
height. Maura often stood on a stool when working in the kitchen, as
did Akeyla. Ellie seemed a little confused by the higher-than-average
counter, but didn't seem to mind.

The box she set down was her camera obscura. The smooth, oiled,
light-ash-toned unit was about the size of a cantaloupe. No seams
showed and even the lens apparatus appeared to have been carved out

of the same piece of wood. Only the lens cap and the slot for her plates marred the exterior.

"A master craftsman made it. A dwarf. I never met him." She frowned and hopped up onto the other stool. "At least I don't remember ever meeting him." She tapped the camera. "The camera and the plates are my seeing stone."

Some seers cast runes or bones. Some read tea leaves. Most used tarot cards. Ellie was the first seer I'd ever met who basically engaged in magical photography.

The wisps, gearwork, and colors her photo showed looked exactly like what I saw when I looked at someone magical, except more so.

Such clarity always came at personal cost.

"Do you think the concealments have anything to do with your camera?" Magic always had a price.

Ellie ran her hand over the camera. "Chihiro once asked me the same question."

She pulled a portfolio out of the bag. "My mother told me that the enchantments were for my protection. That's all I know."

The portfolio shimmered in the sunlight flooding in from the windows and doors. The sigil on the front shimmered and lifted off the material—which, like the sheath she'd had this morning, I could not identify. Was it bamboo? Leather? Cloth? I couldn't tell, nor could I tell its true color.

"Is this how you carry your plates?" The portfolio was clearly enchanted, though no obvious magic swirled around it.

"Yes," she said. "Look at it on edge."

I squatted down and peered across the surface of the portfolio.

A land danced there. A kingdom. A map or a world or—I had no idea. A mirage of a river flowed around the sigil, which stood in the center like a castle. Trees dotted the surface, as did huts. Animals grazed. A bird flew by my face.

I stood up. "Where..." Never in my life had I seen anything so intricate. No wonder I couldn't tell the make of the portfolio. I was looking at a landscape, not a material. "What am I looking at?"

"It's not real," Ellie said. "It's as much a picture as what my developed photos show."

Was it a map of a fae land? A simple picture? An intricately carved magic? All three? This proved fae involvement. Only fae made artifacts like Ellie's camera and portfolio.

I wondered what Sal would have to say about all the fae-touched items in my house. Probably nothing good. She'd have to stay in the truck until I got a better understanding of Ellie's entanglements.

"I have a book." Ellie opened the backpack. "I found it in my library, and thought you might find it interesting." She pulled out the book. "I suspect it's about the Norse gods from a non-elven, non-mundane point of view."

"Rygnyrök" raged across the front of the leather-bound volume in stretched, curled-and-cornered, clawed-out script. Magic coiled off it, but not dark magic—it was aurora magic, not all that different from the red-and-violet magic that popped off the dagger Rose gave me.

The same dagger I'd slammed into Brother's shoulder before he ran off.

Ellie set the book onto the granite with a hollow thump. "Open it," she said.

The book creaked when I flipped it open.

The page was covered edge-to-edge with a script I did not recognize. I flipped to another page. More script. Another page had a diagram and more indecipherable script.

"I have no idea what language it's in," she said. "It's not runic, nor is it a form of Cyrillic. I even looked for a dictionary. My library has a few other books in what looks like the same writing—one titled 'Nyghtmyr' and another titled 'Succuby'—but no translator."

"Maybe that's for the best," I said. "Who knows what this book could unleash." Especially with a title that looked a little too much like "Ragnarok" for my tastes.

"Maybe the elves know," she said.

I closed the book. "If they'll look at it."

Ellie frowned. "Why? Because I'm a seer?"

Seer. Witch. Likely fae-born—the three things that would get someone run out of town the moment they crossed the city limits. That was, if the elves noticed her. Which the concealment enchantments seemed to be stopping.

So a little good came from her isolation.

Ellie hopped off the stool. She looked around again the way she had when she first came inside—as if my house was the most interesting place she'd ever walked.

Her isolation might keep her presence from antagonizing the elves, but the cost was too high. But I wasn't going to lie.

"Seers and witches are not welcome in Alfheim." I pointed at the book. "But that's not it. If I asked, they'd help. It's mostly that I can't ask for help. And I doubt they'd notice the book."

"Oh." She looked down at the floor. "In Tokyo, I could photograph the kami. They never seemed to mind."

"Did you ever talk to one?" Maybe the enchantments were elf-specific.

"They ignored me when I tried. I figured they were just being kami."

I walked around the counter toward the fridge. "I have not been able to speak about you with a single elf. I don't remember, or I simply cannot get out the words." I tapped the fridge door. Maybe food might help her move on from this reminder of loneliness. "I have pasta," I said. "I make a mean meat sauce."

Ellie walked around the counter. She stopped close enough to touch, but kept her hands in her pockets. "Do you have any more info on the vampire that caused the fire?"

"We found a corpse. And low-demons," I said. "They took a friend's cat this morning while we were out investigating."

Ellie closed her eyes. "I'm so sorry. Low-demons are nasty work. They're hard to get rid of."

Hard enough that the elves called a Thing. "Listen, the elves are going to take care of it." I pointed at the lake, and the wider Alfheim area outside. "They sort of go magically nuclear. They did it the last time dark magic got out of control around Alfheim."

71

"Oh," she said again. "Will it affect me?" She reached for my arm. "You?"

Her finger glided along one of my scars.

"Me? Not likely. You? I hope not."

"My cottage pulls me home when I'm threatened. I don't think you need to worry about me."

No matter how much of a relief her words should be, I still worried. And I would continue to do so for as long as I remembered.

But I wasn't going to panic her. "I'm more worried about the wolves. They'll probably all leave town until it's done." I took her hand. "I don't know about you. The last time was intense enough that several mundanes reacted, which is why they don't do it unless they have to."

She nodded.

"They'll cleanse the dark magic. You should be okay," I said. If I could talk to one of them about it, I would. But I couldn't.

She nodded again.

"Come stay with me when they do it. In case," I said.

Ellie wrapped her arms around my waist. She put her head against my chest, and I think she hiccupped. "You can't talk to them about what it might do to me. When it happens, you won't even remember I'm alive."

I hugged her again, careful not to touch the insides of my arms to any bare skin. "We'll figure it out. The wolves seem less affected by your concealments, and once I'm away from the elves, I remember you."

Mundanes were less affected by her concealments. "Ed," I said. He'd talked to her this morning. I let go, pulled out my phone, and dialed.

"Frank," he said. He sounded as if I'd just woke him up, which I might have.

"Do you remember meeting someone this morning? At Lara's? When we talked?"

Ellie bit her lip.

"The auburn-haired seer you were making eyes at? Be careful there, my friend." Ed chuckled.

Ellie blinked.

"Why?" I asked.

"You're the one who raised a witch, not me," he grumbled. "You're asking for trouble."

Ellie walked away.

"I see magic. I know what I'm dealing with."

She stopped at the table and glanced up at me.

Ed grumbled again. "Yeah."

"Have you talked to Arne?" I asked. "Or Benta?"

"I'm going in now," Ed said.

"Have one of them explain to you what they're planning," I said. "Then do me a favor, okay? Ask Arne or Dag, theoretically, if their plans were to come into contact with fae magic—concealment enchantments, specifically—what would happen?"

Ed paused. "Why?"

"Because I asked, Ed." I knew he was tired and grumpy, but I was losing patience. Or maybe the sadness in Ellie's eyes made me angry. "Because if I could tell you more, I would, but I cannot."

Ed sighed. "Fine," he said.

"Do it tonight."

Ed grumbled again. "Fine," he said again.

"Promise."

"All right, Frank. I'll ask your question. Just stay out of trouble. Please."

"I will," I said, and hung up.

Ellie stared at Rose's neatly wrapped notebook. "Maybe I should go," she said.

She wasn't being manipulative. Not the way Benta would have been if she'd said "Maybe I should go." With Benta, it would have been a challenge. The way Ellie stood, the defeated slump to her shoulders, signaled fatigue.

She was tired of the moving. Tired of the enchantments. Tired of making and remaking the same friends.

Tired of being alone.

Just like me. "And leave Marcus Aurelius here all alone with his second favorite human?"

She laughed. "So you're trying to get the sheriff to ask the elves for you?"

"Ed's a man of his word. He'll ask."

"And you want me to stay for dinner?"

"Yes."

"Then I'll stay."

CHAPTER 10

The original log cabin area of my house is now the open kitchen, dining, and living room area. I added the bedrooms and bath when I returned from the Civil War. I'd adopted a child and my home needed to show it. Now, the extra bedrooms served Maura and Akeyla. The loft came in the sixties when I added new electrical and heating systems and needed attic access.

I'd built the hallway from the main area to the bedrooms wide and tall for my own comfort, which, for everyone else, made it "grand." The master bedroom sits behind the living room, and if you lean against the arch between the kitchen and the hallway, and the bedroom door is open, you can see the wardrobe and the foot of my bed.

I figured, if Ellie and I were cooking, that I would put on a long-sleeved shirt to cover the tracer tattoos. I didn't want to accidently brush up against her arm and have her drop a knife or a hot pan, so I dug around for an appropriate shirt.

T-shirts and jeans make up most of my clothes. I'm able to get most of the sizes I need from specialty clothiers without a lot of tailoring. The truth is, I don't have a lot of long-sleeved options beyond my few crisp, white, good shirts.

So I was digging in the drawers for a while. When I looked up, old t-shirt off and in one hand and a long-sleeved one that wasn't too beat-up in the other, Ellie stood in the threshold between the hallway and the kitchen.

She slid a new plate into her seer stone camera obscura.

I pulled the new shirt over my head. When I looked again, she was capping the lens.

I walked out of my bedroom. "The light is better in the kitchen," I said. I don't like people taking my picture. I don't like being reminded that I'm an oddity.

Ellie smirked and waved me closer. "Sneaky candids get me better readings." She looked up. "You okay with that? I don't have to develop them if you're mad."

I tucked the long-sleeved t-shirt into my jeans. "Maybe I should have put on a nicer shirt."

The smirk returned. "And get meat sauce on your best button-down because of me? Nice clothes are for dates."

She was flirting again—and I couldn't help feeling that it was a defense mechanism. My call to Ed probably reminded her of how she might not be welcomed in Alfheim. Did she flirt when life threatened to isolate her again?

Ellie bristled. "I'm sorry for taking your picture without asking," she said, and turned toward the kitchen.

The flirting was most definitely a defense mechanism. Real flirting only happens when a woman is comfortable.

I wasn't surprised. I would not lie to myself about my disappointment, or its weight, but that was my life. Still, I would do my best to make her comfortable, no matter the root of the flirting.

"I'm not mad, Ellie." I followed her around the counter to the table.

She pulled a sheathed plate out of her back pocket and placed it into the portfolio, then drew an empty sheath from her leather satchel. "You have an expressive face, Mr. Victorsson," she said.

Was she mad because she thought I was mad? I chuckled. "The elves don't think so," I said.

Ellie tapped the portfolio. "I took a picture of all the enchanted items." She waved her hand over the tabletop, Rose's notebook, her portfolio, and the book she brought from her library. "Just in case."

None of the magic lifting off any of the objects looked nefarious, nor did they seem to notice each other, the way Sal and the dagger had noticed each other. The enchantments here were low-level natural magic—even the mirage on the surface of the portfolio—and nothing that interacted in a more evolved manner.

But I was glad she'd taken the picture. If her camera lived up to its seer-stone purpose, it would show possibilities in the magic that I could not see in its natural state. "With low-demons around, you could never be too careful. You'll develop everything tonight?" I asked.

"Yes," she said.

I touched the table. "If I don't remember you tomorrow, ask me to look at my phone, then remind me of the concealment enchantments."

She nodded.

"And ask me specifically if Ed learned anything about fae interactions."

Another nod.

"I'm going to figure this out," I said.

She closed her eyes. "I believe you." She smiled to cover up her manifesting emotions: Isolation. Loneliness. Disappointment. Hurt. It was all there.

And she claimed I was the one with the expressive face.

I touched her hand. "The emperor and I will keep you company until we can no more," I said once again. I told her the same thing this morning, when we met.

She stepped into my arms. Stepped in, wrapped her arms around me, and laid her cheek against my chest. "Your shirt smells like the forest," she said.

Maybe the flirting would become a friendship. Maybe not. Right now, I didn't care. "I wear it to chop wood."

She looked up at my face. "I never had a friend until Chihiro," she said. "Never, before her, had anyone tried." She returned to resting her head on my chest. "I really don't know what I'm doing here."

I hugged her closer, carefully minding the tracers in case my shirt wasn't enough, and did my best to be comforting.

Ellie had me utterly flummoxed.

"I don't know what I'm doing, either." I learned a long time ago that what I wanted and what a woman wanted were likely two completely different things.

In my first decades in Alfheim, I learned that most mundanes—and many of the elves—instinctively did not trust a lumbering, ugly giant. Then I joined the Union Army, and learned the true definition of ugly.

Yet Rose hadn't been afraid of me. During the five years we walked the Mississippi back to Alfheim, I carried a happy, carefree child on my shoulders. "Ugly is as ugly does," she used to tell me, before the witch insanity took her.

Maybe I'm overly cautious. Maybe I am the "world's largest puppy," as Benta called me. But I would not state my wants until I knew for sure that the woman in question was okay with the necessary level of emotional intimacy for want-sharing. I wouldn't be scary and ugly.

Plus, every type of magic has its steps.

So here we were, Ellie and I, two uncertain people inside a concealment enchantment that would reset any possible progress on those magical steps each and every morning.

No wonder she was skittish. No wonder she had no idea about flirting and not flirting and personal space—or taking candid photos. She had even less of an idea about how not to be scary than I did.

Ellie tapped my chest. "You promised me a mean meat sauce," she said.

So seers changed the subject as much as elves. But if changing subjects was what made Ellie comfortable, we would change subjects. "Chop onions for me?"

She squeezed my fingers. "Sure."

～

I LEARNED about Chihiro and her language studies while we chopped onions and garlic. I learned about Tokyo while we browned the meat and uncorked the wine. Ellie gave me a detailed account of the natural world of Japan—the mountains, trees, gardens, flowers, rocks, stones, rivers—all the things that kami, fae, and elves love so much.

And all I could think about was that I wouldn't remember any of it tomorrow.

So I took notes. I dropped one of Akeyla's unused school notebooks onto the kitchen counter and I started writing things down.

Ellie found the unicorns and flying horses on the cover cute and entertaining. She tapped a chubby orange-sherbet-colored Pegasus. "Are they real?" she asked. "I mean, like the elves and fae?"

I shrugged. "I've never met one." I've never asked the elves about them, either. Magical animals were more the domain of the fae and the kami than the elves, anyway. "Some of the modern interpretations of the Valkyrie show them riding winged horses." Not that I'd ever met a Valkyrie, either, and I hoped not to for at least another century or two.

Ellie smiled, sipped her wine, and told me that Chihiro has a cat named Maru, which meant *boy*, and was the same silly play on words as an English speaker naming their cat Tom.

I wrote down as much personal detail about her friend as I could, to help Ed in searching. Ellie did not remember Chihiro's address, which upset her, because she'd been in her friend's house a number of times. Nor did she remember Chihiro's phone number, or even in what district of Tokyo they lived.

Her natural magic flared when she tried to remember, and I began to suspect that some of the patterns and forms that looked natural were not natural at all.

I wrote my suspicions down, too.

She told me what she remembered of San Francisco, and the small town outside of Berlin in which her cottage once landed, and the brief two weeks her home appeared in Alice Springs, in the heart of Australia. "It was hot," she said. Then we raised our glasses to kangaroos everywhere.

I drew her a cartoon 'roo. She laughed.

Dinner turned out better than I'd hoped. We ate, and Marcus Aurelius ate his, then padded out to the deck with us to watch the remains of the sunset.

I set my pen and Akeyla's school notebook on the outdoor table next to my wine glass.

My lake-side deck has almost the same square footage as my original cabin's footprint, and includes three levels and spaces. Toward the house, one large table with an umbrella. By the lake, the open area where I sunned my cold morning bones. In the center, a benched area and the table where I now stood. Ellie had camped out here this afternoon while she waited.

I added a bench swing to the center section when Maura and Akeyla moved in. My niece often did her homework out here, rocking back and forth as birds skimmed the lake and the construction crews pounded out the Carlson house.

The swing was big enough for two, even if one of the two was me.

Ellie set her satchel on the table, then placed her camera on top. "This late at night, I need to keep them close," she said.

Seemed the farther away from her the camera was when her cottage pulled her home, the more likely it was to "smack her hard."

She would be vanishing soon, unless she walked home before the pull started. She was not to be around when the enchantments reset overnight, so the magic moved the world a little bit when it wanted her back, no matter her wants or needs.

"We have a few hours," she said. "Most likely."

Seemed the pull back could happen any time between sunset and the night's midpoint, but usually happened closer to the middle than the beginning.

Then this would all vanish. The entire afternoon. The sunset.

Reds and oranges danced over the trees and the water. Frogs chirped. A few fireflies winked on and off over the shore. Marcus Aurelius lapped water from his outdoor bowl and spent his time sniffing the ground around the deck rail.

Ellie took my hand. "Thank you," she said, and hugged me once again.

I was still flummoxed. How many times had she leaned close, or walked into my arms, or touched my hands? But I still was unsure about her flirting.

Benta had not been my only relationship in my two hundred years. When you are lonely, a woman feigning attraction in exchange for protection is good enough.

Was some of what I saw in Ellie a plea? Was it simply loneliness? I didn't think she knew any more than I did.

"Every so often, you get this intense, keen look in your eyes," Ellie said.

I looked away. The Carlson house was dark tonight—no one had come out to check the ruins—so the lake was quiet and calm.

"I'm two hundred years old," I said. "I've seen a lot. I'm just trying to figure out if what I'm seeing now matches anything I've seen before."

"Does that include me?"

I knew she would ask that question. How could she not? Any human would ask the exact same thing.

Marcus Aurelius rooted around just off to the side. He growled, and jumped back, then lifted his head as he hopped up onto the deck.

"Did you find a snake?" I asked my dog. "He has a slithery friend under the deck."

I turned back toward...

The swing. I was on the deck, near Akeyla's swing, with my hand on a notebook she'd left on the table.

"Was I talking to you?" I asked my dog.

I'd been thinking about a woman—and my body carried all the tension that came with thoughts about beautiful curves and loving touches. I frowned and stretched my neck.

"Benta," I said to myself. Who else could I be thinking of? After all these years, thoughts of her still managed to work me up.

I picked up Akeyla's notebook. They would be back on Saturday, so I should probably set the book on her bed. I picked up the pen next to the notebook, too, and held it up.

Akeyla didn't use my good pens. I shrugged and tucked it into my front pocket of my jeans.

I looked out at the lake. Should I go out vampire hunting? After the low-demon incident, Dag told me to leave it alone.

In the aftermath of Rose's death, I learned—the entire town learned—that when the elves call a Thing and tell the non-elves to stay away, one must comply.

Dag told me to leave it be. She told me to sleep. Yet I knew that so much of what had happened over the past few days was because I unwittingly let my brother in. I understood intellectually that the dark, slimy, low-demon magic manipulated me, but that didn't stop the spinning pit in my stomach.

Marcus Aurelius nosed around looking for his snake. With low-demons around, he needed to stay safely in the house.

"Come," I said.

Marcus Aurelius bounced toward the doors. I lumbered my way up the levels and opened the door for him. I set Akeyla's notebook on the table. I'd put it in her room when I got back.

I should drop my tired body on my bed and do my best to ignore the lingering thoughts of beautiful women. I should go to sleep.

I should listen to Dag. But if I could help clean up a mess I made, I should.

CHAPTER 11

Vampires come out once the sun disappears. Their aversion to sunlight is more a metaphorical magic issue than anything to do with UV radiation or needing a good pair of sunglasses, which is why artificial lighting often bothers them as well.

It's not the light. Demons die under the warmth of life and the brightness of scrutiny. It's that simple.

Yet the night was full of life, too. I figured proportion and geometry had their hands in vampire magic—that the retreat of warmth and the expression of decay shifted the natural magic of the world and made demonic movement easier. But I wasn't a magic wielder, so my theories were just that—theories.

I brought my big torch flashlight with me anyway. I figured if I came across Tony or Ivan, I could at least give them nasty headaches.

I trudged along the path from my place across the peninsula to the other arm of the lake. They'd done their damage on my side and were probably looking for new-yet-familiar places to hunt deer and feed on animals.

My flashlight illuminated the path, but not a lot else. The trees and underbrush here soaked up the light. I was walking into a real-life high-contrast relief.

Nothing growled at me. Nothing ran away, or hissed, or chirped. It was as if the lake's animals knew I was coming and stayed out of the way.

I pushed forward into an eerily quiet nightscape.

I could have gone in the other direction, around the lake and toward the Carlson house. My brother's traces were likely all over the burned-out glass-and-chrome remains. But vampires are sneaky in general—and Tony particularly so.

Plus, this was the way toward the meadow, the small one between my place and Rose's Hill, that I hadn't noticed until Rose came to me there. Maybe if I visited again, she would come back. And maybe, just maybe, she might provide some answers.

Doubtful, I thought. Spirits were as vague as vampires were sneaky, though with spirits, their vagaries were often caused by their status as reflections of a living moment, and thus being unable to answer questions. Most weren't malicious.

Rose hadn't been. Ivan's ghost did not seem to be. So I figured I should try.

My brother carried his portal into The Land of the Dead on his person. It moved with him, which was why Arne's first attempt to close all the portals into Alfheim hadn't worked. And when my brother began to dissociate, he was no longer able to control his portal, and could not jump from one location to another. He literally had to run away to save himself.

He also controlled the ash from which he built his clothing.

The ash was the portal. It was the only explanation. When I threw a tracer into The Land of the Dead, when he followed it out into Alfheim, he "grabbed" both the ash and the portal on his way out.

I stopped walking and once again asked myself the same question I'd been asking since he appeared on Rose's Hill: What had my father built? Who had I let in?

The path narrowed up ahead. Two trees loomed over the spot, both with wide, sturdy trunks, but they were close together. The path unwisely pressed between them, though for a normal mundane, the space would be small but not constricting. I had to turn to get through without bumping my shoulders.

My flashlight flooded the area, but the space behind the two trees still sucked up all the light. A massive shadow waited back there, and I stopped again, more to peer into the gloom this time than because of any revelation.

Was I being paranoid? Rightfully jumpy? Nothing back there felt ominous. I pressed through.

There should have been more path. More trees. Maybe a raccoon or a squirrel. Frogs chirping and maybe a few bats flapping around.

I walked into a version of the moonglow meadow. I stepped through the trees into a place that had not been here a few nights ago. An eerily quiet place, one cold and shadowed, much like the pocket realm bordering The Land of the Dead in which Rose's ash-cabin manifested.

I'd walked into a magical bubble—a spellwork mimicking the real world. I turned around. The trees were gone. I stood in the middle of this not-quite-real place.

Opposite me, on the other side of this space that should have been safe—had been safe before—a figure manifested out of the shadows.

Only the more theatrical vampires use circling black mists to mark their exit from camouflage. The prima donnas, as Tony liked to say. In my experience, they also tended to be social climbers with moderate enthralling abilities, and used their beauty and tricks to dazzle as much as they used their demon-given abilities to sway.

This vampire simply stepped out of the shadows in much the same way as an owl in a tree hollow took wing, yet he did not reveal his face —or anything at all about his person.

I was in a place bordering The Land of the Dead with a magical vampire.

Was I looking at my brother? Tony? Ivan? I should be able to tell them apart purely on size alone, but I could not tell if I was looking at a small man up close or a large man in the distance.

And I... couldn't move. I stood in the white flowers under the moon several steps farther into the meadow than I should have been, and I could not move my feet forward or backward. Fireflies buzzed around me. Gnats, really. They were too small to be actual fireflies, and their color was too pale and too sickly to be real. They swarmed. They swirled... like ash.

They pulled back and for a second, for a microburst of a moment, I thought they'd formed up a skeletal horse. But the mirage vanished, and the flies flitted and dashed and stabbed.

One bit my neck and I slapped it away. Another bit my arm. I slapped. More bit my face. Some got into my shirt and bit my chest. They bit and bit and—

My protection enchantments activated. They sprung outward and swatted away the entire swarm.

The vampire on the edge of the clearing raised his hand and the pale gnats galloped through the air to his outstretched fingers, but they didn't stay with him. They separated and swirled and descended onto small animals I had not noticed before.

A raccoon. A rat. A mangy, stray dog. Beetles. Wasps.

Roxy. She bared her teeth and hissed. Then the low-demon-possessed cat took her gnats and ran into the woods.

The vampire at the edge of the woods flickered, and in one blink, he stood directly in front of me.

I still could not tell if he was a small man impossibly close, or a large man some steps away. He looked down at me from behind his shade of ash, but he did not smirk, nor did he feign superiority. He studied.

"This world will be mine," he said. "But do not fret, my brother. Do not wail or gnash your teeth, for I am a just and kind ruler."

He waved his hand and I stopped asking questions. I stopped wondering. I just... waited.

He extended a hand and touched my protection enchantments, then pulled back his fingers as if he had touched a live wire. He moved closer, and peered at the enchantments around me as if he, too, could see magic.

The monster, the vampire-thing, grabbed one of my enchantments. He wrapped the fingers of one hand around its gearwork.

He pulled.

One of my protection enchantments' many pylons unmoored. It lifted off me and out of the protection cage as if he extracted a length of rebar directly out of a bunker's fortifications.

He held out the magical length of protection. Then he smacked it against his thigh.

A pipe appeared. He smacked it again, and a spearhead appeared on one end. Another hit, and the shaft extended.

His free hand snaked through the new hole in my protections and he curled his hand around my neck. "Some of my kind wish to destroy everything and every mundane in their paths. But where does that leave you in the end? With nothing. It is better to learn to farm than to rely on the whims of the world, yes?"

Greenish-black, slimy magic poked at my protection spells. It wiggled in, and under, and once again toward my flesh.

Rage wanted in again, but not *my* rage—the rage of what now controlled my brother's patchwork body. His indignation at being destroyed by a mundane. His anger that his rightful, worldly kingdom had vanished into Eastern European geo-politics. His annoyance that he needed help to claim from this world what he felt he deserved.

My rage erupted from a death interrupted. My rage poured forth from muscles cinched in agony and bones cracked by loneliness.

My brother's rage flowed from the spin of a demon. It had started, long ago, as indignation and self-aggrandizement, as war and murder. As vindictiveness and pure evil. At death, his spirit refused to lose itself to the entropy of The Land of the Dead. His spirit spun, and tightened, and ruptured even magic.

So what I felt now from the low-demon black slime was not a pulling to the surface of my own ignoble faults. What I felt was evil concentrated by the centrifugal force of a long-dead man. I felt viciousness distilled.

He lied about not destroying all in his path. He might do it with flair and handsomeness, but he would crush the world under his heel.

And he would start with Alfheim.

"Who are you?" I asked.

He slammed the end of his newly-formed weapon into the ground. "You know who I am. *Everyone* knows who I am." He stroked a finger across my cheek. "Sleep now, my brother. We will meet again tomorrow."

What would this monster need from me? Hadn't he taken enough? He took advantage when he tricked me into letting him in. He took my dignity with his continued threats.

So what could he want? My blood? My soul?

"Yes," he rumbled. "I want it all."

CHAPTER 12

I dreamed of fireflies over a meadow. Small flies in pale green, or yellow, or in some cases, bruise purple. Each with its trail of fire-like light marking out its path. They danced, the fireflies. They circled and they synchronized.

A mare galloped through the meadow. The flies drew up, and down, and the mare shimmered with their lights. She galloped through the moonglow flowers as a shadow of a horse, a pale-maned beast of discord and grief. Fire trailed from her eyes as a blaze marking her path under the moon.

The fireflies edged away from natural magic into the controlled— they swarmed, but not as a cloud that could be moved by the breeze. They swarmed like gears and knives.

The horse snorted and growled.

Workings and nightmares, I thought, and the piecemeal parts of my body agreed. I am the god of mixing and I knew best when all that is myself agreed.

Nightmares.

Workings....

Someone banged on my door.

I rolled over and opened my eyes. Bright light snuck in between my bedroom curtains, so it was well past sunrise.

Whoever was at my door banged again. "Frank!" a male voice called. "We have work to do!"

The King of Alfheim himself, Arne Odinsson, stood at my tree-side front door and demanded my attention.

I'd been dreaming. Something about nightmares and magic. But hadn't I gone out last night? Maybe I'd dreamed that, too.

Of course I'd dream about nightmares and magic. My dreams never had been, and would likely never become, anything prophetic. They, like everyone else's dreams, were more about sorting the previous day's activities than anything fascinating. I suppose I should be impressed that this one was more poetic than not being able to find cheese at the grocery store.

Arne banged on my door again.

I rolled out of bed and pulled on my jeans, then staggered into the foyer. Arne banged again. "You sleep like the—"

I swung open the door.

"—dead," he said.

I frowned down at the elf who was more of a father to me than the man who'd stitched together my body from the bits of corpses. "Not funny, Arne," I said.

He frowned back and pushed his way into my house. He tried to hide the limp my brother had given him, but he stepped lighter on his wounded leg than his other.

"Still healing, I see," I said.

He dropped his glamour and I swore even his ears scowled his response.

Arne's silver-held, semi-living black ponytail swayed behind his head. His notched ear looked a little more notched, as if my brother had managed to take out yet another bite, and I was pretty sure he had a new scar dipping below the collar of his fighting leathers.

"Why are you asking questions about the fae?" he said.

Arne Odinsson was not a small man by either elf or mundane standards. Many of the male elves were taller and broader than most of the mundanes, and clearly reflected the body types of their Norse heritage. Arne was usually the biggest individual in the room.

Even after two centuries, Arne swaggered as if his subconscious still did not approve of his being dwarfed by my presence.

I usually ignored it. It was what it was, but for some reason, his posturing rankled me this morning. "I have no idea what you are talking about," I said. "Why would I be asking questions about the fae? We had a vampire problem, not a 'prancing through the woods on ethereal hooves' problem."

Arne snorted. "Ed called. Said you needed to know about fae concealment enchantments." He tapped my chest. "Put on your shirt."

I shook my head and walked into my bedroom. "I have no memory of asking Ed about fae anything, much less concealment enchantments."

"Which makes me wonder if the fae are using your brother."

I pulled a t-shirt over my head. "What?"

Arne walked down the hall toward the kitchen. "Why wage your own battles when you can send in a berserker vampire?" he called.

My refrigerator door opened. "By Odin's plucked-out eyeball, you need to go grocery shopping, son."

Marcus Aurelius was circling Arne's legs when I walked into the kitchen.

He held up the one bottle of iced coffee I kept in the door for emergencies, popped off the top, and chugged it down. "Feed your dog," he said.

"Would you like some freshly brewed French roast, Arne?" I asked.

He set down the bottle and tapped the countertop. "What I would like is for this chaos to be done." He waved his hand toward the lake. "I cannot take lightly the possibility of fae involvement."

No, he could not. The fae were, at best, a complication. Having a fae around—even a sweet, kindly fae—was like finding yourself in a pond with a sweet, kindly tiger. Even nice and playful, they could kill with the swipe of a paw.

Never in my life had I met an actual fae, for which I was thankful, but I had seen what they leave in their wake.

Not all the atrocities of the Civil War came from cannons and mundane slaughter. The War disrupted the grounds of several of North America's fae—creatures the Natives and the Europeans alike respected and wisely left alone.

The hills of Appalachia are a thick place, green-blue and humid, and full of life. They remind me of Northern Minnesota, but denser.

Such places attract fae.

I will never forget the screams in the fog. The sounds of splatters, and the gurgling. The low drone like wind through rocks, or the hollow steps of a beast grander than I. We found parts of mundane soldiers the next morning. I thought it a witch. When I returned to Alfheim, Arne told me the truth.

A fae, and probably not a powerful one. Just a creature whose life had been disrupted and who fought back.

Elves were dangerous enough. But they were housecats compared to the fae.

And now we had hints of fae-born concealment enchantments in Alfheim.

"Why would a fae care?" I asked. "It doesn't make sense." I poured water into the coffeemaker.

Arne leaned against the refrigerator. "The motives of a fae are its own." He slapped the door. "We must protect Alfheim."

"Yes…" I said. Everything came back to protecting Alfheim.

He blinked. "You look skeptical." He pulled a can of dog food out of the cabinet and walked toward the opener. "The vampire problem is complicated enough." He fitted the top and the little machine buzzed. "Adding even a hint of fae turns a situation we could have sorted— painfully and probably at high cost, but sorted still—into a free-for-all of infinite impossibilities."

Arne plopped the food into Marcus Aurelius's dish.

"It *cannot* be that bad, Arne," I said. Fae were dangerous, yes, but he made it sound as if the dogs of war had already slipped their leashes.

I glanced at my hound, then at the elf pacing my kitchen. "What are you not telling me?" I asked. Because this had to be bigger than gossip about maybe—possibly—a fae situation.

He leaned against the counter. "Never in my life have I seen a vampire command low-demons." He looked up. "They are base creatures, low-demons. They will devour what they are pointed at, but low-demons are no more controllable than a swarm of rats."

I added the coffee to the maker.

"Only once have I seen them controlled, Frank. On Gotland, before we sailed with our Norse to the New World."

I closed the lid and started the brewing.

"A fae." He stood straight. "A particularly dark fae, one who was truly and utterly insane." He looked at the lake. "He'd thralled a hive of low-demons and set them on the villagers." Arne closed his eyes. "I have seen horrors, as have you, my friend. But this was ghastly."

Ghastly meant bits and pieces. *Ghastly* meant chewed.

Arne stood straight and tapped the countertop again. "The attack on Magnus's horses adds another layer of concern." He pointed in the general direction of the farm and stables.

"Ed told me." Yesterday morning, when I saw him at Lara's Café.

"Three are still missing. Two Percherons and a stallion." Arne shook his head. "It's related. To everything, including the site in the woods." He pointed in the general direction of the creepy place. "I went out with Ed. Benta took us to the body." He frowned. "She is an angry elf, Frank. Be aware."

"I know," I said, and did my best not to roll my eyes.

"There was no more magic at that site. I checked. Benta also checked. We were arguing when Ed got the call from Magnus." Arne nodded toward the forest again. "Mark Ellis took him out to the stables to check. We didn't find magic, but he did."

Arne held up his hand. "This morning, one of the stablehands said something about the 'glow of a hellish fire' around the stabled horses."

"The low-demons," I said.

Vampires always escalated. Always. But Arne was correct; such control of low-demons should be beyond any vampire's capability, and far outside my diminished brother's.

Tony and Ivan, though, were, as Benta said, an enigma. "Are we sure Ivan didn't pick up something from Rose's papers?"

Arne looked up at the ceiling. "Do you honestly think your daughter had that kind of spellwork in her papers?" He shook his head. "All she left were ramblings, Frank. Herbal enchantments and small recollections of dreams. It was jumbled and chaotic, yes, but not sinister. That's why I allowed Ivan to sort and catalog. There wasn't anything there."

"Then why did you destroy them, Arne?" The question popped out of my mouth before I realized what I was saying.

"Because sometimes chaos interacts with the sinister, and Akeyla's father was up to no good."

He was right. Left alone, Rose's artifacts weren't anything sinister. Tony and Ivan, by themselves, might be vampires, but they were fine and helpful for several decades before my brother showed up.

The world had had its balance, but once that balance tipped, it flopped over into its hellish handbasket.

"Dagrun told me not to allow Tony and Ivan into Alfheim. She said that yes, we can help those in need. Yes, we can offer opportunity. But with vampires, the risks were too great." He shook his head. "I did manage to keep them under control and in a good place for seventy years."

Like Magnus, sometimes Arne took the role of his namesake too seriously. With Magnus, it was fertility and prosperity. With Arne, it was his status as the All-Father. Arne walked among the peoples of the world. He gathered. He gave knowledge. Sometimes that led to betrayal.

Though with vampires, that coming betrayal should have been obvious. But who knew who was at fault here—Tony, Ivan, or Brother? Tony and Ivan might have made it another seventy years without an issue if my brother hadn't shown up.

But what-ifs were not the issue at hand.

"A house burned last night," Arne closed his eyes again. "Outside of town. I fear the vampires have moved up to mundanes."

And here I chose to sleep last night, instead of hunt.

Arne pointed at my nose. "You saved Akeyla. Yes, we suspected they would escalate but no one thought it would be this fast. And none of us can fight exhausted. We thought we had a day or two to reset the magic."

The coffeemaker hissed its final drip. Arne pulled two mugs out of the cabinet by the stove. "Most of the wolves went out to the body site. No one picked up anything." He set the mugs on the counter. "I didn't pick up anything, either, though it sure looks like a land through which evil has walked."

Arne's body posture said that if he had been a mundane man, he would have shuddered. But he was neither mundane nor a man, and the smell of evil did not faze the Elf King of Alfheim.

Arne poured himself a mug, then poured one for me. "Which is why Ed telling me you were asking about fae concealment enchantments piqued my interest."

"What's the plan?" I sipped at my hot coffee and soaked its warmth into my cold, stiff fingers.

"We're going to take care of this *today*," he said. "Axlam and Maura are taking the kids to the Duluth Aquarium. They're going to spend the night at that hotel with the water park."

"Good," I said.

"Remy and Gerard are taking the adult wolves out of town, along with a couple of the less-powerful of my kind. They will all be out by mid-morning."

A cleansing like this worked best at daylight maximum—not railroad time noon, but the point of the day when the sun stood directly over Alfheim. Nothing burned out dark magic like the light.

"Sun's out today," Arne said. He pointed at the sky outside. "No clouds to inhibit sunshine."

The less-magicals, if caught in the blast, might not fare well, hence the leaving. "What about the mundanes?" I asked.

"There are seven thousand people in my town," Arne said. "Odds are one or two of them carry trace magic."

Witch blood, an old family curse diluted by centuries, a brush with a kami on vacation—it could be anything. Which meant we would have issues. "Ed and his family need to be out of the area you're cleansing, too." I said pointing at my neck to indicate where a vampire had given Ed his scar.

Arne nodded. "I'll call him. He won't be happy."

I shrugged. "Tell him that as soon as it's safe, we'll need him in town to help assess if we have anyone with a hangover."

"Aye." Arne looked up at me. "And then there's you."

"I think I should stay with you," I said. I carried magic, but I wasn't inherently magical. "I survived the last re-alignment just fine."

"You weren't carrying tracers or asking about forgotten fae concealment enchantments."

True, I thought. "You don't want to face my brother on your own," I said.

Arne gripped my arm. "I was hoping you'd say that."

Should I be happy? Probably not. But I would do my duty. "Where am I needed?"

Arne set his mug on the counter and for a second watched my dog paw at the doors to the deck.

"I'll let you out in a minute," I said to the emperor.

"I already cleaned the glamour around The Great Hall." Arne stared out at the lake for a long moment. "I did so right after your brother found his way in." He looked up at me. "I want you to come in. If you're inside the glamour when we clean the town, you'll be close *and* safe." He curled his large-yet-elegant hands around his mug. "Then follow us. Use your magic-seeing abilities. Make sure we catch everything and it's all gone."

"There's a possibility I won't see anything." Beyond the oozing, oily rage, Brother's magic was invisible.

Arne took another sip of his coffee. "I trust your gut reactions even if you don't see something." He set the mug down again. "I will take the elder elves and start at the river outside The Great Hall glamour." He looked up at me. "We will clear the town first, and re-establish our boundaries. Then we'll move into the surrounding territory."

The elves were about to reset the town's magic. Essentially, if I understood correctly what they'd done last time, they would flare the magic of The Great Hall into the surrounding territory. Glamours would reboot. Equilibriums would be upset. But the resulting wave of magic would burn away small, incompatible magicks, and mark larger ones for extraction.

Such re-alignments upset the natural order of a wilderness. Many animals were likely to panic. But we would be rid of whatever dark magic fed the vampires and the low-demons.

"Come in by noon." Arne rubbed his shoulder as he re-glamoured. "Make sure you have your phone," he said, and walked toward my front door.

I turned back to the counter and my coffee once I heard the door shut.

I looked up.

A woman stood on my deck.

CHAPTER 13

A beautiful dark-auburn-haired woman stood outside my French doors, close enough to look in. Her dark blue shirt hugged her breasts and accented her lovely face and skin.

Marcus Aurelius wagged his tail and barked a greeting.

My dog wasn't upset by the stranger. When she waved at him, he turned in a circle.

"When did you make a friend?" I asked. Maybe she'd found him when he ran off a couple of days ago.

I opened the doors. "Um, hello," I said. She was even more beautiful up close. "Are you one of the new neighbors?" The Carlson house wasn't the only new cabin going in.

My dog jumped up and licked her face.

I pulled him off. "Sorry about that. Marcus Aurelius usually has better manners." I waved at the kitchen. "Come in. I need to leave soon, but you're welcome—"

"Frank," she said, and took my hand. "You told me yesterday that if you didn't remember who I am, that I was to tell you to look at your phone."

"Remember you?" This woman was unforgettable. Natural magic danced along her skin and gave her a shifting, calming shimmer that reminded me of silk in wind. And she was perfectly shaped. Perfectly curved. Her eyes glowed with life and intelligence.

She smiled and touched the outside of my arm. She tipped her head and bit her lip. "I will never grow weary of seeing you make that expression," she said.

"What?" She wasn't making any sense.

"Frank." She cupped my cheeks. "We met yesterday. Look at your phone."

She touched me like an intimate—like a good friend or a lover. Like I should pick her up and place her behind me so she didn't drown in any of the coming magical waves.

What was I thinking? I didn't know her, no matter what she said. I couldn't. Nothing could make me forget so thoroughly that I wouldn't remember *her*.

Unless...

"Are you the source of the concealment enchantments?" Was this woman a fae?

I stepped back. The beauty could be a glamour. Magic fluttered around her, but none of it looked spell-like or controlled. It all looked natural.

Which could be part of the glamour.

Shock drained the color from her face. Her eyes grew huge and she bit her lip again. "I..." She wiped at her face. "I developed the plates. I thought you would want to see."

She pointed at the kitchen table.

Two books sat in the center, one Rose's notebook, and one I hadn't noticed earlier. A book with obvious magic flickering around its binding.

I hadn't noticed it, and neither had Arne. "How long were you outside?" I asked.

"I saw you and the elf come into the kitchen," she said. "Marcus Aurelius noticed me when I came to the door."

"You *are* the source of the enchantments." Was she a dark fae? No malice flitted off her the way it would if she was dark. "Are you thralled by the vampires?" A thralled fae would explain a lot. "How the hell did the vampires thrall *you*?" I ran my hand over the top of my head. "Maybe my brother was more powerful than I thought."

"*Frank!*" she said. "You don't remember me because the enchantments hide me from the world! They reset every night and I vanish from the memories of the people I meet. Every night. Every person! Always." She pinched her lips closed. "I had a friend where I lived before. You wanted to help make sure she was okay. Yesterday, you *did not* think I was evil!"

She swung her backpack—*my* backpack—off her shoulder. I recognized the distinctive stain on the front pocket.

"That's my backpack," I said.

She ignored me, moved the two books on the table to the side, and opened the pack. "This is because of that elf, isn't it? Your friend asked him about the enchantments and now he's all riled up." She set a portfolio on the counter. "He looked important. He's the King around here, isn't he? Arne, I think you called him yesterday. Arne Odinsson, the Elf King of Alfheim."

She set a wood box on the counter. "I should have told you to stop. I should have said to leave the elves out of this because they always get their knickers in a twist. That's what my mother told me."

She opened the portfolio. "But no, I trusted you. I thought 'He's sincere. He's handsome. He's better than that.' Yet here we are, you backing away from me like I'm a troll when all I wanted was..."

She slammed her mouth shut and looked away.

Her words swirled in my head: *Trusted you. He's sincere. He's handsome.*

"You think I'm handsome?" I'm an idiot. All the words I could say and it's "You think I'm handsome?" that falls out of my mouth?

Idiot.

Her lips thinned. "I came back this morning, didn't I?" she said.

I'm in love, I thought. Which was just as stupid as asking if she thinks I'm handsome. So, so stupid. I know damned well what being in love means. It takes a lot of work. More work than an argument with a possible fae whom I don't know.

And I hadn't acted this stupid around a woman since... I'd never acted so dumbstruck. Except around Benta when she first took an interest in me. And Sally, until I figured out she just wanted a protector.

Still, this new woman could be enchanting me.

Her expression tightened as if she'd just read my mind. "Go find your phone, Frank Victorsson. Look at the background."

I swear she was frustrated enough to throw the salt shaker at my head.

"Okay, okay." My phone sat on the charging station next to the hallway along with my keys and a pile of mail.

"Where's your notebook?" Ellie asked. "You were taking notes last night. The one with the unicorns on the cover."

"Why would I be taking notes in one of Akeyla's school notebooks?"

She sighed a full-on, dramatic sigh of frustration. "Fine," she said. "I don't know why I thought that this time would be any different from any of the rest." She closed her eyes.

"It's not my fault I don't remember you," I said.

She stared at me for a long moment, then tapped her chest. "My name is Ellie. Ellie Jones. It's sort of nice to meet you yet again, Frank Victorsson, son of Victor Frankenstein. Your dog and I have met before."

Ellie rubbed Marcus Aurelius's head. "He, at least, is a good judge of character."

"That's not fair," I said.

She knew about my father. Only a few close friends know about my father. People I trust and whom I consider family. "How do you know my father's name?"

Ellie pinched the bridge of her nose. "You told me. I know you're two hundred and seventeen years old. I know you found the emperor by the side of the road and decided to adopt him. I know the elves consider you a son and that you are happy here in Alfheim."

I frowned.

"Check the dishwasher. Does it look like you had company last night? We made pasta and a lovely meat sauce. The wine bottle is in the recycling." She pointed at my garbage can.

My frown deepened.

"I'm not going to argue with you, Frank. This anger you feel is because of the dissonance between what the deep parts of your brain remember and what the enchantments allow to surface, and I want none of the bluster it causes."

Ellie smacked the table.

How many times in her life had she dealt with what I'd just put her through? The disbelief? The questioning? The arguing? She'd presented pretty clear evidence that we had, in fact, spent time together.

I learned a long time ago that my size and scars frighten people—mundane, elf, or fae-enchanted alike. That fear gives social interactions a cutting edge that sliced away connections, so I learned to be calm. I learned to moderate. And I damned well learned that the last thing I wanted or needed was a woman—any woman—to think I was a self-absorbed, angry jackass who acted more like a child than a grown man.

I learned to apologize. "I'm sorry," I said.

Ellie sighed again, but her face softened.

"I am." I walked toward the table. "I think you're right about there being a dissonance." Nothing made good sense and it was making me fidgety.

"You're going to do exactly the same thing tomorrow," she said.

She was coming back tomorrow.

I smiled.

Ellie grinned and shook her head. "The enchantments make people forget about me. They make for a lonely life, but that's all."

"I really am sorry," I said. "We have a vampire problem right now. That's where all this is coming from. Arne's…" What did she say? "… got his knickers in a twist."

Ellie chuckled.

"He's a good man. The elves here are good people. They'll help, once we get the vamps under control."

Ellie took a sleeve from the portfolio. "I took photos yesterday. I thought maybe my seer ability might help with the vampire issue." She slid what looked like a daguerreotype photo from the inside. "I took this one of your kitchen." She pointed at the two books.

I knew how I came to have Rose's notebook—Ivan gave it to me before Arne destroyed all her papers. But the other book, the one marked with Norse designs on the cover, was just... there.

"I brought that one yesterday," Ellie said. "I'm actually surprised it didn't go back to the cottage when I did." She tapped the Rygnyrök book. "I think I know why."

She slid the photographic plate across the table.

Like any true daguerreotype, the silver-coated copper plate onto which the image had been captured shimmered in the room's ambient light. And also like any true daguerreotype, the image floated just above the surface.

But this plate was different. The shimmer wasn't simply a reflection of my kitchen's overhead halogens. Magic wove in and around the silver coating.

"That plate is enchanted," I said.

Ellie frowned yet again. "I really wish you remembered how this works." She tapped her chest. "Seer." She tapped the wood box. "Camera obscura seeing stone." The she tapped the plate. "Daguerreotype photographs showing what I need to see."

"Isn't a camera a bit complicated to be a seeing stone?" Never in my life had I met a seer with a "stone" that resulted in readings which needed developing.

"Frank." Ellie's shoulders tightened. "We talked about this yesterday. Honestly, I don't know what the elves have taught you, but most seers do *not* use the simple, theatrical stuff like casting bones." She sniffed. "You want a good reading? You need a good tool."

Ellie tapped her camera.

I *humphed* and pulled the photo across the table.

"I know you see magic," she said.

I peered at the plate. Magic arced between the books like the curves of a magnetic field.

I glanced at the actual books. Natural magic flickered around both, but nothing sputtered. Nothing snipped or howled or did anything at all suggesting the two objects noticed each other.

She set another plate on the table and pushed it toward me. "This is the photo I took of the Carlson house across the lake."

The remains of the Carlson house stood out in the center of the photo as a gray, shadowed, pointy mass in the midst of the natural curlicues and branches of the woods. Dusty, ash-like wisps and flecks rose off it as if it were still on fire.

Magic wisps.

I peered through the door. Across the lake, the charred chrome façade looked sad and dirty, but not charged with magic.

I picked up the photo. Some of the wisps carried definite enchant-ment indicators—gearwork-like spell symbols, faint sigils, and gradi-ents in luminosity—all of which concentrated into points of darkness around the property.

Points that also formed up into a larger, meta-level enchantment.

Ellie pushed a third plate across the table. "I took this one at dawn this morning. It's the meadow where I met Marcus Aurelius."

I knew the meadow. It wasn't far from the death-creepy place where Benta and I found the body. It was also where I'd seen a ghost.

"Rose came to me there." My adoptive daughter had seemed more whole in her ghostly state than she ever had been when she lived.

And... "I think I had a dream about that meadow last night." Dreams came and went, but what I remembered—horses and fireflies —carried anxiety and fear. And usually, if a dream shifts toward a nightmare, it's something I remember.

I picked up the plate. Specks floated in the air over the patch of wildflowers that filled the center of the meadow.

The fear tightened. "I wish I could remember what I dreamed."

Ellie touched my hand. "It wasn't me. The enchantments don't usually interfere with dreams."

"I know," I said.

Ellie pulled another sheath from the portfolio, but thought better of it and returned it to its spot. She flipped the page and removed another sheath instead.

"When I was waiting for you to return yesterday, I walked around your property. That gate, the one with the wine bottles, reflects light beautifully. I took a photo of it and the side of your house more for artistic reasons than for a reading."

She slid the sheath's photo toward me. "I think you'd better look at it."

Arne fought my brother on my property two nights ago, before the Carlson house burned. I set down the photo of the meadow and picked up the photo of my house.

Yes, I saw magic, but I had no idea the level of magic—around not only the gate, but around my house in general. Arches. Sheets. Flares… and the speckles again.

"My camera reveals not just present magic, but also past and future magicks it feels I need to know about in order to make a good reading." She pointed at the plate. "The photo is confusing."

"I'd say," I said.

"The magic around the gate is different." She held the photo on edge. "See? It's on a different level of the photo's holographic imprinting."

I nodded.

"I think that magic is yet to come." She set the photo down again. "But this magic here," she pointed at the damage on the side of my house. "That's in the past."

More speckles concentrated on the layer with the past-magic than the future-. "My brother did that," I said.

Now she nodded. "I think my camera can trace your vampire brother." She tapped the first photo. "I think the interactions between the books are also yet to come." She tapped her finger again. "I wish I knew why."

She tapped the other photos one at a time. "I can see where your brother's been. I think, maybe, I might be able to see if he's going to be in a specific location."

She closed her portfolio. "At the very least, I can show you where he's been, so the elves can clear his dark magic."

This woman whom I did not remember clearly had been in my house yesterday. She was also the one whom the fae enchantments concealed. Not a fae. Not my brother. Ellie Jones, seer. "I asked Ed to ask the elves about concealments yesterday, didn't I?"

"The less magical a person, the more they remember during the day. He must have talked to the Elf King before nightfall. Your elf friend remembers being asked, but not why. Ed won't remember me today, but he might remember talking to the elf."

"And I told you to tell me to look at my phone?" I walked over to the charger again.

And there, right on my phone's screen, was a smiling Ellie hugging Marcus Aurelius.

"Arne's wrong," I said. "We aren't dealing with a dark fae."

"*You're* not," Ellie said.

When I looked up, she waved it off. "I brought several undeveloped plates."

I needed to figure out how best to use this development. Alfheim now had a seer. A powerful one, too, from the quality of her photos. But come tomorrow, no one would remember.

"I need to call Arne." I pulled up his number.

"It won't do any good," Ellie said. "The more magical, the less I register. You ran a series of tests yesterday. I could be standing right next to the King and he would walk right past me."

"That's an intense enchantment."

Ellie placed her portfolio and her camera back into the pack. "The enchantments that conceal me from the world are powerful and intricate." She zipped up the pocket. "Such is my life. I just…" She gripped the pack. "Call him."

I dialed Arne's number.

He answered. "Frank," he said.

"I…" I couldn't remember what I wanted to say. "There's…" I wanted to tell him a beautiful woman was standing in my kitchen, but the words wouldn't come out.

"Frank, is everything okay?" Arne asked.

"Yes, yes," I said. "I..." What should I say?

Arne paused. "Is this about the—" He stopped talking. Arne, it seemed, was as confused about the reason for my call as I was.

"Don't worry about it," I said, and hung up. I held up my phone. "It's always like that? There's no way around the restrictions?"

Ellie shrugged. "This is the first time I've landed in a heavily magical place. Mostly, I'm with mundanes, so I don't know."

"And mundanes remember you for the day, but forget you overnight?"

"Yes."

"Looks like Ed is the only way to get information to the elves."

Ellie wrapped her arms around her chest and looked out over the lake. "We should be careful. I suspect that if the enchantments become aware of Ed's circumventing ability, they will compensate."

I tucked my phone into my pocket. "Probably." Strong magic often responded more like a living thing than not, as Sal had demonstrated many times.

Ellie looked me up and down. "I don't want anyone else to get hurt because magic moved my world again." She glanced over her shoulder at the Carlson house. "But if I can help, I will. I need to do something good with the hand I've been dealt."

"Can you develop your plates on the fly?" I doubted she had an instant daguerreotype camera. Magic could compensate for a lot of missing technology, but everything had its limits.

Ellie shook her head. "I need my developing room and equipment." She pointed at the backpack. "My camera doesn't need extensive exposure time, like the originals. It responds more like a modern, high-speed digital single-lens reflex camera."

At least we wouldn't need to stand around on a brace for six minutes while the light seeped into the system.

Arne had asked me to come into The Great Hall. "The elves are going to release a cleansing spell," I said. "It will affect you." I pointed at the spells on my head. "It'll affect me." But would it affect the concealment enchantments?

"What should we do?" she asked.

"Have you ever dealt with a major outside enchantment?" Maybe she had an experience that suggested precedent.

"Once I caught an accidental backwash from a kami." She pointed outside. "The magic flipped me back to my home even though it wasn't yet time. Hurt like hell, too."

"Did it affect the concealment enchantments?" I asked. Would Arne's cleansing be enough to disrupt what hid her from the world?

She shook her head. "No. They just pulled me out of the way."

"Your seer abilities would be very helpful right now," I said. "To check for dark magic after the spell goes through."

"I think so, too."

"Are you willing to risk it? Being pulled back? I'm going to try to get you through The Great Hall's glamour." I picked up my keys.

My extra house key sat in a bowl next to the charger. I looked at Ellie.

Arne said he trusted my gut instincts. I should probably trust them, too. I picked up the key and walked over to her.

"Here," I said, and pressed the key into her hand. "It unlocks the doors." I nodded at the French doors out to the deck.

Ellie looked down at the key. "Thank you," she said as she tucked it into her front pocket.

"In case," I said.

She picked up the backpack. "The worst that could happen is that I vanish."

She was taking a huge risk. "Are you sure? I don't want to get you hurt."

She touched my elbow. "If I can help, I will."

CHAPTER 14

Marcus Aurelius nosed his way between the truck's seats and under Ellie's elbow. He whined and nuzzled, and tried his best to crawl onto her lap.

"This again?" she said to my dog. "You're too big, love. You'll knock the gearshift."

He whimpered and settled his snout alongside her thigh.

"I think he remembers you," I said. Either he remembered, or my dog's excellent sense of character was in overdrive.

"Chihiro had a cat but he didn't seem to care one way or another." She rubbed Marcus Aurelius's ears. "I wish you could talk."

"Maybe I should get a parrot. Wouldn't be my first." I turned onto the highway that led into town. "African Grays are quite intelligent." And a bit moody.

Ellie grinned. "Other than Chihiro, you're the first person I've met who wanted to find a way around the enchantments."

"That can't be so." I could think of several people who wouldn't give up just because of the puzzle of it all. And then there was Magnus Freyrsson, whom I'm sure wouldn't give up until he found a way into her bed.

Ellie snorted. "I can see on your face exactly what you are thinking, and yes, I have learned how to gauge a man's motivation." She shook her head.

I opened my mouth, but closed it when she laughed.

"Every man motivated solely by sex stopped trying after the first day of forgetting," she said.

Good, I thought. "All of them?" I asked.

"Every single one." She poked my bicep. "Except you."

Were we flirting? I was pretty sure we were flirting. "That's because I'm not solely motivated by sex," I said.

She laughed again and rubbed my dog's ears.

"Wait." A realization dawned. "Did we...?" Because that was something I did *not* want to forget.

Ellie laughed again. "No. Gotta get through that first round of forgetting, remember?"

She was definitely flirting. A beautiful woman was flirting with huge, lumbering me.

She wiggled in her seat. "You make a mean pasta, Mr. Victorsson. I will happily dine with you again."

I didn't know what to think other than to thank last night's pasta-cooking Frank. Seemed I was my own wingman.

Ellie laughed again. "We learned I cannot touch the tracers on your forearms or the protection spells on your scalp." She pointed at my head. "Yggdrasil seems okay."

So the concealments interacted with elven tracer magic. "I'll remember."

She chuckled. "One of these days, you will. I have faith."

One of these days, I'd look back on this and be very happy, indeed, but only if Alfheim survived its current vampire scourge.

I turned onto the county road leading into town. We'd drive by Lara's Café, then either around town on the main service road, or through downtown, before getting to The Great Hall.

Ellie looked out at the trees. She might like downtown. It was definitely more picturesque than the ditches and warehouses.

But we should concentrate on our task. "Have you ever dealt with a low-demon?" I asked.

She watched an apple orchard go by. "Once, in Germany. The kami in Japan are... how should I describe it? Militant, maybe? About non-native demons. Any whiff of manufactured maliciousness and the kami immediately take care of it. So not a lot of low-demons around."

"What happened in Germany?" I asked.

Ellie rubbed Marcus Aurelius's head. "It wreaked havoc in the village. I think it managed to influence one of the angrier, more selfish members of the community. He was hurting people." She frowned. "I got a picture of it one evening outside the tavern just before my cottage pulled me back."

She frowned as if she couldn't remember what happened. "It was gone the next day."

"So someone dealt with it?" I asked.

Ellie frowned again. "I suspect so. My follow-up photos indicated that it had been cleansed from the village." She sighed. "The more you ask me questions, the more I'm sure the enchantments mess with my memory, too."

"We'll get it sorted," I said. We had to. Even without the threat of a vampire scourge, having a powerful seer around whose life was pock-marked the way Ellie's was would ultimately lead to problems.

Secrets always did.

"Oh!" Ellie pointed up the road. "Could we stop at Lara's on the way back? I'd like to take a muffin home for breakfast tomorrow."

I almost asked when she'd been to Lara's, but the answer seemed obvious. "Sure," I said.

Ellie smiled.

I lost my train of thought. Right there, as we drove by Lara's food truck, right out in the open under the sunny morning sky, I utterly forgot about vampires, and magic, and nuclear options. None of it seemed important.

Ellie looked away, but I could see her smile reflected in the window's glass.

We were about to crest the hill leading into Alfheim's main down-town district. Main Street was a wide boulevard, with one lane of traffic in each direction, a center turn lane, and parking on both sides.

The sidewalks were also wide, and several shops and restaurants spilled outside. Alfheim's many art galleries also displayed local wares, as did our elf-run tattoo parlor.

The beading store caught Ellie's attention and she looked over her shoulder as we passed by. "We can stop there, too," I said. "Tomorrow, after the elves have cleaned the town. Remind me and I'll bring you in."

"Thank you," she said, but looked away again.

Was I coming on too strong? Even when I'm trying to be friendly, I can come across as scary. "I mean if that's okay with you," I said. "If you're comfortable with it. You'll just need to remind me." I shrugged. "And remind me not to be so much of a jackass about not remembering when you come by."

Marcus Aurelius nudged her elbow.

"He remembers you. Just point that out." I knew I needed to stop talking at her. Talking at someone was not how you made them comfortable with you.

"Okay," she said.

We stopped at the main light in the middle of the downtown district. Red, green, and multi-colored blown-glass apples glistened in the window of the gallery on the west side of the street. Posters of some band called Barston Flood covered the windows of the second-hand book and record store on the east.

All the tables out in front of the café across the side street were empty. I glanced at the gallery. No one browsed the art. I looked over my shoulder. No one walked up and down the street, either. Besides us, no in-use cars waited at the light, nor were any visible in my mirrors, or down the cross street, or ahead. Only empty, parked cars waited at the curbs.

A firefly popped out a bright, yellow-green light directly in front of my truck's windshield.

During the day.

"It's mid-morning," I muttered. Fireflies did not come out during the day, and never downtown.

Ellie peered at the stores. "Where are all the people?"

"There should be tourists," I said. Besides the stores, downtown had three small, quaint hotels. One even had a housecat for every room. Dag liked to talk about how all three were always full, even in January.

Three more fireflies sparked in quick succession in front of the truck.

"Did you see that?" I pointed at where the lights had appeared.

Ellie shook her head. "No..." she said.

Was it magic? Had the elves already started cleansing the city? It wasn't noon yet.

The stoplight changed.

My truck wouldn't move. The engine sputtered and the gears ground, but the vehicle wouldn't inch forward.

Several more firefly-like lights popped in an arc around the truck. An actual arc formation, as if following a geometry.

I wasn't looking at fireflies.

"What do you know about fairy lights?" I asked. This wasn't fairy lights, either. Not in town. Not away from nature and in the bright sun. This was something else entirely.

Ellie peered out into the street, but it was obvious that she didn't see anything unusual. "I take it you are seeing magic I am not."

I pulled out my phone and dialed Arne. "Something is wrong," I said to Ellie.

Vampires might be predators, but they weren't natural predators, and so used malice and subterfuge to trick their prey.

And right now, my entire body tightened because nothing said "trick" like fake fairy lights.

Malice and subterfuge had beaten the elves into the center of town.

CHAPTER 15

"Do you think it's low-demons?" Ellie asked. "In the middle of the day?"

Arne's number rang and I peered at the gallery and its red, green, and multi-colored glass apples. The moment wiggled—not shook or changed the way vision changes when you realize you're blinking. It wiggled like magic.

And for a split second I thought I saw a woman reaching out to touch one of the apples.

"It's magic—" My phone stopped ringing. "Arne, I—"

The high-pitched indicator tone burst through my phone's speaker. "We are sorry. Your call could not be connected at this time," a robo-voice said.

I looked down the street. Alfheim's Main Street is about five blocks long and visible from one end to the other. We were at the light two blocks in. Up ahead, the road curved toward the river and The Great Hall.

To each side, the streets moved away from the downtown district toward more trees and the town's mundane houses. Behind us, the buildings we had already passed.

Fairy lights popped and shimmered in all four directions. They arced and swirled, twisted and gyrated. They swarmed, but not in a natural way. They swarmed as if controlled.

I'd dreamed about fireflies. My mind, like everyone else's, used dreams to sort clues. So what was my subconscious sorting?

Except I was beginning to wonder if it had been a dream. I went vampire hunting. I had a "dream." I woke up in my bed the next morning.

"Ellie," I said, "do you think it's possible to enchant individual bits of ash?" Rose used the ash to backfill her spells, but as far as I could tell, the ash itself wasn't enchanted beyond its container.

But the ash in question was from The Land of the Dead and territories adjacent.

"Maybe enchant one small bit, then use a duplication spell?" Ellie said. "But that's complicated magic only someone well-practiced could achieve."

"And if you enchant enough of it, what do you think might happen?" The dagger in my brother's shoulder kept him from moving in and out of The Land of the Dead, but that didn't mean it kept The Land of the Dead from moving to him.

Rose used the ash to make a facsimile of her world. With enough enchanted ash, my brother could do exactly the same thing here. Right now. In the middle of Alfheim.

Ellie pointed down the street. The fairy lights concentrated. Around them, the air thickened. She pointed. "That's not fog."

Not at this time of the day. Not billowing like gray-green smog—and not moving at the speed of a volcanic eruption.

"Roll up your window!" I slammed closed all the vents on the front of the truck.

Ellie hit the button to close her window. I reached behind our heads and closed the vent in the back windshield. "Stay down," I said to my dog.

The wave hit the truck. We rocked. The vehicle groaned, and the engine cut.

Ash splattered the windshield and hit the roof like hail, though it hung more like a mist than a cloud. I could still clearly make out the shops on either side of us.

And for another split-second, I thought I saw someone open the gallery's door.

"You see magicals, but they don't see you, correct?" I asked.

"Yes. It's as if I'm behind a screen and they don't see me."

Ash. Concealments. The cutting off of communications.

"My brother wasn't diminished." I slapped the steering wheel. "We thought that the dagger dissociated him somehow and that he became lesser because his parts were no longer working together."

This was not the work of a diminished vampire. Hell, this was not the work of a *vampire*. Something told me that the ash, the stink, and the thick, gray haze were all part of a fettered, angry, and thickly-concealing dark magic. How it looked, how it smelled, how the elves thought they could cleanse it, meant nothing.

She sniffed. "Do you smell that?" She sniffed again. "Sulfur."

I inhaled. My senses were more acute than a normal mundane's, and I should smell the same scents as Ellie. "I don't smell anything," I said.

She pulled out her camera and loaded a plate, then pulled a satchel out of the pack. She threw the strap over her head and tucked the bag against her side. "More plates," she said. "It'll hold the camera, too."

Marcus Aurelius whined.

I looked down at my dog. I'd just brought my trusted animal into a place likely infested with animal-possessing low-demons.

"You were supposed to be safe inside The Hall glamour," I said.

Ellie placed her hand on the emperor's head. "There isn't a low-demon in any of the Realms with the spine to take you. Huh, boy?"

He *woofed*.

"Good," she said. "But you stay next to your people, okay? Right by our sides."

He *woofed* again.

"You are a special dog." She gave him a quick hug. "You are special to me and I want you to be safe."

They had a bond. A strong, one, it seemed. Ellie and my dog understood each other.

Her expression softened when she looked at my face. "I like you, too," she said. "Even if you're argumentative in the morning."

The flirting was going to kill—

A wave of déjà vu hit me. I'd thought the exact same thing before. I didn't remember when, but I *knew*.

The flirting was going to kill me.

"Ellie…" I said, and reached for her hand.

She wove her fingers into mine. "Thank you," she said, and leaned close—but yanked back. "Frank!"

I spun around just as *something* hit the driver's side window. It sucked at the glass, then pulled off with a wet slurp just as fast as it had hit in the first place.

"Was that a bat?" Ellie asked.

Bats didn't slurp.

Nor did bats have white, glowing teeth and red eyes.

"A low-demon," I said.

The yellowish haze hanging around the buildings thickened. It rolled upward and outward like a New England fogbank.

The low-demon that took Roxy produced some shadows, but nothing like this. Nothing this dark and… heavy.

The fog had a weight to it. Real weight, as if the atmosphere literally thickened. As if Alfheim had been transported to a world where gravity operated differently.

The second bank hit us hard enough that the truck rocked again. This time, the stink of sulfur hit my nose. Ellie sneezed and held her hand over her nose. Visibility outside dropped to zero.

Something hit the side of the truck bed. We rocked again, but my truck held.

Ellie pulled her camera out of her bag and pointed it at the windshield. A flick of her wrist and she exposed the magic of the ash to her seer-stone.

I cranked the key to start the engine. I'd be driving blind—if the truck started—but I had to try to get us out of this.

The engine sputtered.

"Is it working its way into the lines?" Ellie said. She pulled her t-shirt over her nose and mouth.

I tried again. This time, the truck started.

Another bat-creature hit the window, this time on Ellie's side. She screeched and jumped, but thankfully didn't panic.

Marcus Aurelius stuck his head between the seats again and let out a low whimper-growl.

"Whatever happens, you stay with Ellie, okay?" I said to my dog. I tapped his head, then tapped Ellie's arm. "Protect Ellie."

He barked a response.

"It's like a volcano erupted," Ellie said.

We were about ten yards from the buildings on either side of the truck. In front of us, the cross street. I couldn't see the streetlight. What if this was all an illusion and we were broadsided if I pulled out into the street?

Something landed in the bed. Something big enough that the entire vehicle bounced on its shocks.

A growl echoed from the truck bed. Marcus Aurelius growled in response. Ellie pulled her camera and her bag tight to her chest.

And I did the only thing I could—I accelerated hard into the intersection.

Whatever was in the back skidded toward the tailgate. I braked and it skidded toward the tool chest.

I accelerated again, but this time, I pulled the wheel hard to the left.

It hit the side of the bed. A yip-howl erupted through the ash-fog, then the clacking of claws on my truck's metal bed.

Another bat-creature hit the windshield. I accelerated into the truck's spin.

Whatever was in the back stopped skidding. It hit the back windshield—headbutted, actually. Wide, red eyes, a long snout, and pointed ears hit the glass.

A wolf. A *were*wolf.

Ellie screamed.

Did a low-demon get one of the wolves? I slammed on the brakes and the wolf skidded toward the tailgate again.

She pulled out her phone. "I have Ed's number. I'll call. You drive."

Except I'd lost my bearings when I put us into a spin. We could be facing The Great Hall. We could be facing back toward the outside of town. Or a parked car could be inches from Ellie's door.

She dialed. "Sheriff Martinez? You don't know me. Frank Victorsson gave me your number. He said I can trust you."

The wolf in the back of the truck hit the window again.

"Ed!" I yelled. "The—"

The phone's screen cracked. Sparks popped off it, and the cab filled with the acrid smell of burning wires.

Ellie dropped it next to the backpack between her feet. She swore and stomped, but the pack ignited.

"Frank!" She slapped and stomped, but nothing stopped the flames.

I pulled her over the gearshift and into my arms. "Don't let go once we're out. Got it? Stay with me." I hit the steering wheel. "Marcus Aurelius! Protect Ellie!"

I flung open my door and dropped us both into the ashes of The Dead.

CHAPTER 16

Ellie clutched my belt with one hand and Marcus Aurelius's collar with the other. Her bag with her camera and portfolio of plates hung around her torso. She kept her t-shirt over her nose and mouth—as did I.

My truck crackled. A sickly orange glow outlined the windows. It burned but all we smelled was the ash.

The wolf in the truck's bed howled—and Sal yelled.

She'd been silent and hidden up until now. Concealed, as if she was trying not to be noticed by anyone, including me. But now she was alone in the back of my burning truck with a possessed werewolf.

I couldn't tell who it was. I couldn't pick out markings or size, but something told me that I wasn't dealing with Gerard or Remy, or any of the older wolves.

Ellie had told Marcus Aurelius that no low-demon had the spine to take him. Same applied to the wolves. The wolf pacing in the back of my truck was likely one of the newbies.

"I need my axe," I said.

"What?" Ellie said.

I could see her, and Marcus Aurelius's back, and the glow of my burning truck, but that was it. The world was descending into the flat, dark gray of soot and ash.

Smog-filled, twilight gray.

"It's not just low-demons and possessed werewolves we need to worry about," I said. "The vampires can walk in this."

Ellie nodded.

I fished out my phone and quickly pushed it into the pocket of her jeans. "It'll probably burn," I said. "But if we get separated, I'm hoping your concealments will protect you enough that you can get a call out."

She nodded again.

"I want you to stay exactly where you are, okay? Right here with the dog. Don't move. I need to get my axe."

Ellie pulled her t-shirt off her face and quickly stepped close.

She kissed my jaw.

Something locked into place inside me. Something vital and real and not at all the puppy-dog romanticism that Benta once used to make me feel small.

All those parts I need to share, all the offers of touches and the needs for intimacy, they rotated like magical gearwork. They turned. They clicked. And those parts of me became Ellie-shaped.

I pulled her tight against my chest. "Hold onto Marcus Aurelius," I said, and let go.

One stride and I was at the side of my truck. I gripped the bed's wall and vaulted into the back.

"You know me," I said in the best canine-soothing tone I could muster. "I won't hurt you." Though even a newbie wolf could do me great harm.

Heat pushed through the soles of my feet from the heating metal of the truck bed. Ash worked grit into my eyes and my nose, but I needed to keep my senses about me. I needed to track the wolf.

Somewhere by the tailgate, in the billowing ash cloud, a beast growled.

I backed against the tool chest. It, like the bed, had heated to painful, and I quickly flipped open the top.

I keep a hammer in the chest, a tape measure, a socket set, and a few other tools. Most of them are old and well-used. A few, such as my hatchets, would probably be valuable on the antiques market.

But none of them were inherently magical. Or so I thought.

Sal sang a bright blue flash of sound and light. The tape measure flexed and snapped. The hammer vibrated.

Sal had enchanted the tools in my box.

I picked up the hammer. Violet energy danced along the handle and over the steel head, down my arms, and onto the tracer enchantment tattoos.

I usually carry six tracers, three on each arm. I'd lost one to Brother when I tossed it into The Land of the Dead and my throwing arm now only carried two. The hammer's energy touched the closest —and changed.

If the hammer left, I wanted to follow. I wanted to chase after it, to know where it was, and to always carry it back to the toolbox.

"I think I love you, Sal," I said, and whipped the hammer over the side of the bed in the direction opposite from Ellie and my dog.

The wolf yipped and jumped out of the bed, following the purple arc of the hammer's light as it vanished into the twilight gray ash. I caught sight of his tail—black, fluffier than most of the wolves, and with three concentric light-gray rings at the tip.

Mark Ellis.

"That wouldn't have worked if he had full command of his faculties," I said.

Sal agreed. The enchantments flowed off the other tools and back to Sal, and I got the distinct impression that I needed to pick her up and carry her to safety.

"I got you," I said, and swung her over my shoulder. I hooked the hatchet to my belt, then grabbed the spool of rope from the corner of the box. Heat radiated through the rear windshield from the smoldering cab, but the truck was off, and nothing sparked, so it wouldn't explode. We wouldn't be escaping in it, though.

I closed the toolbox. Time to return to Ellie and Marcus Aurelius. Possessed werewolves weren't the only danger in this fog.

Off in the distance, Mark yipped and whined as if someone had hurt him.

I froze and listened.

Nothing moved in the ash. Nothing flittered. Nothing groaned. Ellie stood still, as did Marcus Aurelius.

I could just pick out her outline. She pointed into the fog in what I suspected was the direction of The Great Hall.

Horseshoes make a specific metal on concrete *clomping* sound when a horse walks the streets. It starts with a tick, then quickly shifts into a deeper strike. This happens with each of the horse's footfalls, and it makes a particular sonic pattern, depending on the size and speed of the animal.

Three horses were approaching, one in front and two behind. The patterns of their clomps suggested that the two back horses were moving slightly faster than the lead, probably because the lead was bigger than the other two.

Three horses were still missing from Magnus's breeding operation, including two Percherons. They were show horses, and beautiful, massive beasts. Like Magnus himself, they were enchanting.

They were also some of the few horses stabled at Magnus's operation that were large enough for me to ride comfortably. I'd learned a long time ago that even if the elves' Fjord horses—and elven Fjord horses were larger and faster than their mundane relatives—could handle my bulk, neither they nor I were comfortable.

I'd always favored at least a Percheron, and if one was available, a Clydesdale or Shire horse.

So I knew the sounds of the approaching hooves. I knew the lead horse.

My brother was larger than I. He would need the largest horse in the area.

The clomping slowed. A horse's head appeared out of the ash.

Magnus called the stallion Blodughofi. Everyone else called him Bloodyhoof. He stood nineteen hands at the shoulder, and his pedigree included elven Fjord and Shire horse—he was Magnus's latest attempt at a new breed. Like his Fjord ancestors, he carried the black midline through his mane and along his back, as well as a black tail. But his feathers—the long cuffs many of the larger breeds carry—were the same shimmering red-sorrel as his coat.

His eyes glowed with hellfire, and when he tossed his head, the flames trailed.

The dark magic my brother had brought with him had turned Bloodyhoof into a nightmare stallion.

The horse tossed his head again, and snorted.

I glanced over at Ellie. She held perfectly still, and had pulled Marcus Aurelius onto her foot so he pressed up against her leg in what I assumed was an attempt to keep him inside her concealment bubble.

But what if "no magical notices me" didn't extend to dark magic? To vampires?

I readied Sal on my shoulder.

Bloodyhoof stepped forward. His neck came fully into view, but not his rider.

"Brother," a deep, large voice said. One that sounded like my brother's voice, but more clipped. More constrained. Whatever occupied that body now seemed more civilized.

Not that a vampire could be in any way civilized. But they could pretend. They could use manners and refinement as camouflage to hide among the mundanes, but also as an easy glamour.

Nothing allows a monster to walk among regular people of the world better than riches and beauty.

"You are not my brother," I said. I had family. A sister. A niece. "You might have been built by my father, but that does not make us kin."

He laughed—a deep, resonant laugh which, if I hadn't known what I was looking at behind the veil of the ash, would have been fetching.

My brother's body was handsome. The only scar he carried looked more like an artistic tattoo than anything hideous. His face was well-proportioned, as was his frame, even if he did stand significantly taller than my almost-seven-feet.

He was a beautiful monster. A dazzlingly huge mountain of all the things mundanes find enchanting.

And whatever part of him had taken over after his dissociation clearly understood what enchantment meant.

The mist swirled and a shadow of the rider emerged from the ash like a relief on stone. The shadow pulled his legs up and under himself, and in one smooth, quick moment, he jumped to squatting on Bloodyhoof's back like a rodeo trick rider. He braced himself—I couldn't see how, but he held out only one arm. The stallion whinnied, but stayed still.

My brother stood.

I was still in the bed of my truck, but I lost his head in the fog.

"We have business, you and I," he boomed.

Behind him, the other two horses whinnied.

"Tony! Ivan!" I yelled. "He will turn on you! You two must understand your own natures well enough to know what's about to befall you." Perhaps sowing dissent might fracture my brother's power.

The giant standing on the back of the stallion laughed again. "The one you call 'Tony' is my true brother," he said. "We are bound by blood."

Whatever he used to stabilize himself slammed into the concrete. Metal shrieked.

My brother used his stabilizer—it had to be a pole of some kind—to vault off Bloodyhoof's back.

He landed on the truck's hood. Metal groaned, and the front windshield cracked with a loud shrieking that echoed through the swirling ash.

The power of the landing washed over me—and cleared some of the air between me and my brother.

He crouched on the hood of my burning truck, the shadowed figure, with one hand on the metal and the other to his side, gripping a staff so tall its top vanished into the ash cloud. His face was still shrouded, but not the armor he'd fashioned from the soot in the air. This armor glowed a dull, dead red as if he'd mixed in the blood of all his victims.

Plates and guards sheltered his shoulders and neck. A breast plate protected his chest. Individual guards protected his arms and legs.

The dull red of the pieces farther from his dead heart brightened. They pulled in on themselves, forming a pulse-like line, which moved to the next piece in. Then that piece "beat" and sent another pulse inward. Then another, until the symbol on his chest shimmered with all the hate this creature carried. Until all that anger, all that motivation—every ounce of the psychosis that allowed this thing to care inside The Land of the Dead—lit up a symbol I recognized.

We had never met, when we both walked Europe. At the time, I stalked my father in a vain attempt to force a rectification of my pain and isolation. But I'd heard rumors. I'd seen bodies. I'd met one or two of the sniveling-type vampires, the once-men and -women who existed solely for the use and enjoyment of their master.

At the time, I lived in the shadows. I hid. And I read history.

I recognized the crest on the creature's breastplate. I knew exactly what it meant.

The thing on the hood of my truck stood. The ash moved around him as if it was as much a part of the body in front of me as the stitched-together parts of vampire corpses that constituted its frame.

The lightning-bolt-like scar snaked from his cheek to his jaw and under the pulsing, undead, ash armor. His black hair shimmered with a fake life. His eyes mirrored to the world the forces that kept his body animated.

He towered over me, as he had the last time I met this body; now, with the boots and armor, he might have reached a full eight feet in height.

I shouldn't be surprised. I should have suspected that when he dissociated in the Carlson house, one of his constituent parts would take control.

But I never expected that part to be the voivode of Wallachia, her High Prince and her ruler. I never expected Vlad Tepes, the man so terrifying that even in death, his viciousness gave the uncaring of The Land of the Dead purpose. The man whose ghost had whipped up the demons who became the first vampires.

126

His armor pulsed again, and I realized the staff wasn't a staff.

It was a pike.

I stood with only the burning cab of my truck between me and Vlad the Impaler, the creature Western Europeans knew by another name:

Lord Dracula.

He grinned. "Hello, Brother," he said, and swung his pike at my head.

CHAPTER 17

I dove over the side of the truck's bed. I instinctively held Sal between the side of my head and the sweeping growl of Dracula's pike, but I knew it would do no good. Sal could take one, maybe two hits. That pike, whatever it was, wherever he'd pulled it from, was magical beyond the talking elven battle axe I carried.

It was magical beyond the point of the dagger still in his shoulder.

Sal screamed at the remains of the dagger. She pushed and she pulled, and my balance pushed and pulled right along with her.

My dive over the side of the truck bed ended with me dropping unceremoniously onto Main Street, with Sal skidding into the haze in the direction of Ellie and my dog.

Rocks bit into my hands and rashed my cheek and neck. I groaned, but pushed off to run for Ellie.

The ash screamed. It wailed and it shrieked and the pike pierced the concrete directly in front of my face.

My brother—*part* of my brother, the strongest part by every possible measure—stepped out of the haze and wrapped his hand around the shaft of the pike.

Behind him, in the twilight fog, I could just make out Ellie's outline. She still held Marcus Aurelius by the collar. He twisted and shook, and leaned against her leg, but he kept quiet. Sal sat on the ground at her feet.

Ellie balanced her camera against her chest by using the strap of her bag to hold it in place.

Dracula looked down at me. "I have many brothers," he said. "Many children."

He slid his hand down the shaft of his pike as he squatted, and tentacles of ash burst around his fingers like pixie-wraiths. "You are the son of Victor Frankenstein," Dracula said. "The man who breathed life into your body is the same man who breathed life into mine."

I was my father's first draft. Dracula was his bigger, stronger, smarter, second.

His fangs extended out of his mouth and over his lower lip. "Such delicious life," he said.

Behind him, Ellie capped her camera. Marcus Aurelius yipped. She gently touched my dog's snout and shushed him. He whimpered, but quieted.

Dracula continued to grin with his yellow-blue, sulfur-on-fire fangs out and ready to slash.

He was oblivious to Ellie and my dog. Utterly unaware of their presence.

The concealment enchantments were doing their job even inside this pocket of The Land of the Dead: hiding Ellie—and whatever was right next to her—from a highly magical creature.

They could escape. She could walk in any direction and get out of the ash cloud and get away from this vampire.

Slowly, she stepped over Sal and moved closer. Not away. She moved herself and Marcus Aurelius close enough that I could get a read on her expression.

She understood the implications of not being noticed. She knew she could run. But she tucked her camera into her bag and leaned closer to listen.

"How far around the town does your ash-caused twilight extend?" I asked as I stood. I wiggled my shoulders with as much bravado as I could muster, mostly to hold his attention just in case he caught the emperor's scent.

Dracula mirrored my movements right down to the shoulder reset. "What makes you think this is the town, son of Victor?"

I was correct. We were in a pocket borderland.

Ellie shook her head. She waved her hand through the haze and mouthed "too much magic."

She didn't think they could get away.

Dracula cocked his head as if listening. "Where did you toss your wood chipper?" He scowled. "It used its magic and helped you send away my puppy." He tapped his fingers on the pike's shaft. "It allowed you to pick it up." He tapped again. "This body remembers that axe."

Ellie had moved away from Sal, and now the vampire remembered that I'd taken the axe out of the toolbox.

She stepped backward.

"I don't know what you're talking about," I said.

He looked around, and continued to scowl.

Maybe, like the combined personality whom I had called Brother, the Dracula persona inside the body in front of me wanted to talk. Isolation made anyone chatty, and there was nothing more isolating than being an indistinguishable part of a whole.

"What have you done here?" I asked.

Dracula's hand tightened on the pike. The ash-made pixie-wraiths slowed around his knuckles, ducking and biting like tiny vampire bats.

He didn't seem to notice.

"You are using fae magic," he muttered.

I glanced at Ellie. She stood over Sal and backed away farther, her hand still on my dog's collar. They stopped in almost the same position where I'd left them.

Dracula looked over his shoulder. "I smell you, little elven axe." He lifted the pike's tip out of the concrete, then slammed it down again. "I *will* fracture it into shards," he said.

Ellie knelt. She balanced the camera again, and slowly reached out her hand toward Sal.

Which was a bad idea.

"Touching that axe isn't possible unless you have its permission," I said.

Ellie pulled her hand back, and stood again.

Dracula chuckled. "I will not *touch* it, brother. I will shatter it into tiny little pieces."

"Where are the elves?" I asked. "Where are the people?"

"The elves are, right now, scrambling to counter the seeping infection from my little burst boil in the center of their town." Dracula waved his hand and inhaled. "I smell them." He opened his eyes and inhaled again. "Four of them move outward along the cardinal directions around this point."

I glanced at Ellie. She nodded.

"They're going to cleanse your fogbank right off the face of all the Realms," I said.

Dracula laughed. "I certainly hope so."

Ellie's eyes widened. She nodded again.

Off in the haze, a horse whinnied. Tony's voice followed, then the sound of Bloodyhoof retreating.

Dracula looked away as if watching them go. "Unlike you, son of Victor, I realized *how* that witch had enchanted the ash." He winked. "I think my realization had something to do with my affinity for the small, creepy things of death and decay."

"You still cannot walk in the day, nor can you move through The Land of the Dead with that dagger in your shoulder, so you enchanted the ash to build a version of it here, the way Rose enchanted it to build a version of her house." I waved my hand through the thick air. "Thing is, it's still a boil, as you said. It's still not real and it's still isolated. How will this help you get what you want?"

His hand shot out. He had me by the neck before I could react. "I thought you were fast." He twisted his head and peered at my face. "How is such a dead thing so alive?"

One of the horses clopped up.

Tony, dressed in armor almost identical to Dracula's, looked down at us. "It is almost noon, brother," he said.

"I thought I was your brother," I choked out.

Tony reined the blue-black Percheron gelding around. "Why are you playing? We need him in position. The elves are about to open their floodgates."

"Radu thinks our discussions are a distraction," Dracula said.

"Radu?" I asked. "Is that your real name?"

Tony—Radu—smirked down at me from the back of the show horse that was his stolen mount. "I am Radu the Handsome, younger brother of Vlad the Impaler."

Dracula grinned.

I sniffed. "That's one hell of a better story than a Russian Cold War spy, Tony," I said.

Tony slapped his reins across my cheek. "You will not survive this, corpse," he said. His horse snorted like Bloodyhoof, and hellfire bled from his eyes.

"Won't be the first time I didn't survive," I said.

Dracula chuckled again and cupped my face with his hand. "I like you."

Tony huffed.

Behind him, the other horse whinnied.

"We need to be in place," Tony said.

Dracula let go of my face. "It's almost noon." He turned his face upward as if feeling the sun on his face. "Time to energize the base, as they say."

"What are you doing? What's happening here?" If I got him to talk about it, Ellie might be able to get to Ed, and Ed might be able to get to the elves.

The other horse clopped up.

Ivan looked down at me over his hooked nose. "Mr. Victorsson. Are you well?" he hissed.

I opened my mouth to respond, but thought better of it. Ivan never asked questions. Ivan used questions to provide answers.

He looked out over the fog. "Strength, yes?" he said. His horse pawed at the street. "Like aggregate in concrete." He chuckled and walked his horse backward into the ash.

132

Dracula watched him go. "Do you know why Roman concrete still stands after millennia of abuse, and the pathetic mix they make in America can't hold up even a decade?"

Why were they talking about concrete and building materials? "No," I said.

Dracula tapped my forehead. "They mixed the ash of Vesuvius with the blood of a sacrificial ox." He flicked my forehead this time.

"I don't understand," I said.

Dracula laughed. "You expected me to explain our plan in great detail, didn't you? Radu warned me." He patted the haunch of his brother's horse.

I glanced over at Ellie. She continued to hold Marcus Aurelius but she'd wiggled an arm out of her t-shirt. She pulled the shirt over her head next, and pulled it out from under the strap of her satchel.

What was she doing?

"Brother," Tony said. "Listen."

Dracula let go of my face. He took a step to the side and cocked his head. "So they've figured out their pet jotunn is the center of this spell." He inhaled deeply. "The elves are frightened."

Tony grinned. "Ivan, take your place."

"Good. Good." Dracula grabbed the rope and quickly tied my hands. The hatchet, he dropped to the street. "Let the games begin."

He whistled. Bloodyhoof trotted up and, like the magnificent stallion he was, threw his head and snorted hellfire from his nostrils.

Dracula tied the rope to the pummel of his ash-made saddle. "I have questions, son of Victor," he said.

I looked back at Ellie. She'd taken off her shirt and dropped it over Sal.

A loud, painful bell tone blasted through the ash-fog. The air vibrated. I cringed. And Ellie dropped to her knees onto the fabric-covered axe while wrapping her arms around Marcus Aurelius's body.

I blinked.

Alfheim bustled around me. People sat at the café tables laughing and sipping their lattes. Others poked at the gallery's art. Another pair walked out of the second-hand book and record store. My burning truck had vanished, and the intersection stood clear.

I was in the exact center of the intersection, equidistant from the buildings. The streets ran due north-south and east-west, and directly overhead, the sun pulsed down warmth perpendicular to the world.

There's a geometry to the universe. A geometry that often either amplifies or suppresses magic.

The elves picked noon because it would amplify their cleansing spells.

My brother spoke of sacrificial oxen. Of blood spilled to amalgamate the ash and the aggregate into an unbreakable concrete.

How could he make his bubble real?

He had the ash. I was pretty sure I was the ox.

The world wavered again, and about ten feet away, to my side, Ellie and my dog appeared. She said something I could not hear, but I thought I understood: The elves' cleansing spells reset glamours. They clicked over all enchantments, and set everything back to default.

Which meant she was about to vanish. The spell would sweep through and reset her concealment enchantments and the beautiful woman I was just getting to know would be thrown back to her cottage.

I'd forget her again.

Underneath Ellie's knees, Sal did her best to cooperate, and to not scream in agony. The concealments were no more compatible with Sal's magic than was the dagger in Dracula's shoulder.

But the woman and the axe had a plan, and even though they burned each other, they would not be deterred.

Ellie pulled my huge dog as tightly against her body as she could, and—

Ivan appeared. Not the vampire, but the ghost man, the version who had been helping me on and off since my brother first stepped out of The Land of the Dead. Ivan with the curly brown hair and the wide, human eyes. Ivan, who must have died centuries ago.

He looked to me, then at Ellie, then back to me. He held up his hand.

Ellie, my dog, and my axe disappeared.

The real world vanished with them, and the ash and smoke of Dracula's pocket borderland returned. Reality—and Ivan—both turned their ghost backs to me. Ivan swirled with the smoke and ash, but he took up a defensive posture between Dracula and someone who was no longer with us.

Trust, touched my mind. *Trust that you are loved.*

Loved, I thought. Why did that matter now? All sacrifices were loved. That's why they're sacrificed.

I looked away from Ivan just as Dracula ran his pike through my chest.

CHAPTER 18

The Norse believed in nine realms. Everybody got a place—fire and ice, gods and men, elves and giants. It was a free-for-all of home-granting, but no one engaged in that unseemly practice of mixing.

And we all know how unseemly it is to mix up one's worlds. Not only is it bad form, but it often caused monsters.

But the real problem here wasn't the mixing. The problem was the human inability to distinguish a solution from a state change. Asgard to Vanaheim, that's just one set of gods to another. It's tribe to tribe. Alfheim to Jotunheim, that's elf to giant, magical to magical. Again, tribe to tribe. No issue there. Mixing requires stirring, but stirring takes a lot less effort than actual change.

Real problems start when you change a state. Fire to ice. Living to dead.

State changes were changes from one state to another—where a person becomes a ghost or, in my case, a corpse becomes a living man, or an unstable bubble becomes a real borderland to The Land of the Dead—which require actual energy. Spellwork. Knowledge. Planning.

Blood.

My blood.

The head of Dracula's pike pierced my skin. It pushed through my muscle into my breastbone. It hit my heart.

Time slowed—perhaps physically. Perhaps not. But the muscles of Dracula's self-serving, self-aggrandizing smirk moved as slowly as the pulse of his armor's beat.

He'd skewered me with his Vlad the Impaler impaling pike. He'd shoved it into my chest and now he was proud for taking from me the life I'd built for myself. Proud that he'd stolen my blood. My body.

I was about to die for a second time.

Dracula pushed me backward until I slammed against the infernally hot side of my burning truck's bed. The heat screamed from my skin to my kidneys to my bones, and caused much more agony than the piercing tip of the pike.

I dropped to my knees. The pike should not have made it through my protection spells. It should not be sticking out of my flesh.

I looked down at the drab, coarse grayness of the pike's metal. It went into my chest too smoothly, and with too much familiarity.

Dracula howled. The pike parted my heart and separated my spine. It punctured my back and punched into the steel wall of my truck. The head continued away from me, angled downward, and rammed through the axle and the drivetrain, and the shaft slid through my body, then through some more, as the head of the seemingly-unending pike ground into the concrete of this shadow-place's Main Street.

Dracula impaled my *heart*. I should be dying again.

But breaths made it past the pike. Blood continued to pump. What started as shocked agony became the dull ache of too much enchantment.

I touched the pike. It felt like real, cold-forged iron. My truck's metal bed transmitted heat that should set me ablaze ... but it, too, had passed beyond the shock. My skin did not blister.

Maybe I just thought I was pinioned to the ruins of my truck with a pike in my chest.

The truck's frame had warped where Dracula had landed on the hood, and the windows were blown out. Its metal had crushed and extended, and somehow formed a giant steel skull.

The roof had collapsed and pulled the side windows up to form the eyes. The rear window had collapsed into the nose cavity. And the bed had rounded and elongated, and was now the open maw of a dead man's head.

I was skewered to its side like an olive on a toothpick notched between two teeth.

Dracula grinned like the metal death's head behind me. "The rarer the animal, the stronger its magic." He released his hold on the pike just as his armor pulsed again. "And you are the rarest of them all."

Not even Dracula's body was as fantastically unlikely as my own. Vampires were built for immortality. I was simply built.

Dracula's armor pulsed, but in the opposite direction it had before. Magic flickered outward from his semi-heart, to his torso, to his limbs —and jumped to the pike.

My heart contracted and condensed. It yanked and balled up, and all of me—all my body and soul and every part of me that understood all the versions of magic—condensed, yanked, and balled with it.

My large bones diminished. My thick muscles collapsed. I felt as if I'd become, in that one pulse of a moment, nothing more than a mote of dust.

Or a flicker of magical ash.

The pulse hardened into a weight in my chest. I sucked in my breath, my mouth wide open but my throat still as tight as it had been before the pulse. I wheezed, then gulped, and tried to raise my hands to my throat, but they stopped midair, on either side of the pike through my chest.

Dracula watched with a finger on his cheek and his other hand on his elbow. Then he looked around as if expecting the ash in the air to respond. When it did not, he frowned and wiggled the pike.

I gulped in air again just as the truck-skull shook violently.

The weight let go and flowed away—and took my five remaining tracer enchantments with it. They lifted off my arms and melded into the magic rolling off my body.

The ring of a sigil formed under my feet. It shimmered and glowed as all magic did, except this magic glowed pale and sickly—and slimy where it touched me. It lifted off the ground, then burst outward away from the truck in an array of vectors.

And out in the ash cloud, out away from me and the truck and the vampire, things groaned. Things howled and screamed. Raccoons. Rats. Slithering things. Roxy.

Things slapped like wet steaks against rock.

Cracks opened out there. Cracks I could not see beyond the burst of magical light.

"What..." I panted.

Dracula grinned. "We timed the formation spell to the elves' reset." He waved his hand through the still-thick air. "They made their world anew. We made this place new at the same time—and permanently attached it to Alfheim."

He pointed out into the ash. "We are establishing several entry points. The underlying spells of your tracers will call out to my children the same way the one tossed into The Land of the Dead called out to this body." He pointed in the other direction. "Ivan is handling the openings now."

The vampires were using me to stabilize their platform so they could open gates.

"Where..."

Dracula extended his arms and twirled around. "The world! All the places and all the vampires." He patted my cheek. "We amass until night falls on your special little elfdom."

"The elves will..." I panted again. "... stop you."

Dracula shook his head as if I was the dumbest of his pupils. "Radu!" he yelled.

Ash churned. A low, almost-subsonic growl vibrated the entire area, and Tony literally manifested out of the fog.

"Brother," Tony pulled off his gloves just as his pulsing Dracul armor pulled a slow beat up his arms and legs toward his ice-cold heart.

"Our guest thinks his elf friends are going to stop us."

Tony shrugged. "Their cleansing spell swept our ash into piles." He pointed outward at the cracks in the world. "Pulled it all together in convenient bundles for easier cleaning."

"It's concentrated now." Dracula leaned closer. "And with you here, as hard as concrete." He grinned. "Great for building thresholds."

They weren't countering the sweeping part of the cleansing spell. They were counting on it to pull all the enchanted ash together into places where its weight would rip a hole between this borderland and the real world.

And then they were using me to counter the second part of the spell—the actual cleansing—to hold open their holes.

A new pulse moved from Dracula's core out to his limbs, but this time, he lifted his hand above his head. His fist disappeared into the ash-mist, but the pulse did not. The sigil reformed around my feet, and with a dramatic whipping motion, Dracula swung his hand down into the floating magic.

The spokes brightened with pale slime.

Out in the ash the cracks in the world screamed and widened, but this time there were new openings. Sunshine flitted into the ash-cloud borderland Dracula had built. Just a little. Just enough to make Tony cringe.

"Brother, please," he said.

Dracula opened his mouth and leaned into the pain, then waved his hands and jumped twice, like an athlete walking off a sprain.

"When night falls, we will open wide the jaws of my pets onto Alfheim." He gripped the pike.

I knew the coming pulse would rip through me like a bullet. I knew that I would coil inward as it pulled my soul inside out.

I gasped first, then the spasms snapped through my muscles. The swirls in the ash blanked out. I lost my vision.

Tony slapped me. "Ivan says he needs to stay conscious," he said.

Dracula ran a finger through the blood of my wound. "It's not so bad," he said as he tapped the pike. "It's part of you."

Part of me?

I'd gone out last night looking for him, but he'd found me. He took my blood. He fed it—and ash—to low-demons. I remembered him reaching into my protection spells. "You built this pike from my protection enchantments."

He tapped my cheek again. "You are a smart one. I *do* like you." He rubbed the blood around my wound, then poked his finger into the hole.

He stuck his finger into his mouth.

His face curled up as if he'd tasted rotten meat. "You taste like the dead," he said.

Behind him, Tony rolled his eyes. "The elves' spell requires a consistent counter," he said. "We will have..." He stepped close and peered at the wound. "... forty-eight hours until Mr. Victorsson fully bleeds out. He has remarkable healing abilities, which is a boon for us. They will increase the time it takes him to finally die a true death. The longer he suffers, the longer the gates stay open."

Something flew by in the ash-mist. Something fast and wet-sounding. Tony ducked.

Dracula scowled. "Disgusting low-demons," he muttered.

"They are *your* pets, brother," Tony said. He looked up at my face. "Ivan wishes to check your alignment."

I was in the center of a spell, one that fed on the energy of the elves, so of course my alignment with the universe needed checking. The borderland itself would need to be in alignment, as would every internal gear and pulley.

Tony walked three paces directly out from my body. "We leave you now, my dear friend. We have an army to rouse."

Dracula's armor pulsed, but thankfully he did not force the energy through me. "The elves' land is beautiful," he said. "So many fat, happy mundanes. So much vacationing wealth. It's a vampire's paradise."

Tony frowned. "The winters leave much to be desired when you are already cold blooded. Correct, Mr. Victorsson?"

I opened my mouth, but only a pant would come out.

Tony returned his gloves to his hands. "Would you like to check out a bodice-ripper from the library? To pass the time?"

He punched me in the center of my gut, then immediately grabbed my sides, so I would not flinch too much.

"Can't have you getting too far out of alignment, can we?" Tony chuckled as he stepped back.

Dracula whistled. Bloodyhoof and Tony's black gelding galloped up. Both horses tossed their magnificent manes.

Dracula patted his beast's neck, then absently tapped the pike. "And here they thought I would come with a large sword."

He mounted Bloodyhoof. "Thank you, Brother, for your sacrifice," he said, and reined the stallion away.

Tony mounted the gelding. "Thank Mr. Freyrsson for his breeding efforts." He, too, patted the neck of his nightmare beast, then he rode away.

I was alone, left impaled against a skull made of modern life, with my body impaled on a pike made from the magic that was supposed to protect me.

I waved my hand through the ash cloud hoping to clear enough visibility to see the far end of the pike, but no matter what I did, it was too far away. I could try to slide myself up, but the end was likely a forged node meant to keep me from sliding off. I needed to know what I was dealing with before I tried that avenue.

A new slow, almost-sub-sonic growl rolled through the ash. The pike vibrated, as did the truck-skull.

The inner circle of the sigil manifested below my feet.

This time it did not rip through me with the same agony as the others. The same crushing, yes. But perhaps my body was beginning to get used to the vampiric magic draining away my blood and soul.

A smaller, slower horse clopped through the ash-mist as if she did not want to be part of this hell any more than I did.

A white shadow in the ash appeared. I'd been correct—Magnus's white Percheron mare approached. Her muzzle manifested out of the cloud first, then her braided mane.

Her troll-like rider leaned forward. "Hello, Mr. Victorsson," vampire Ivan hissed. "Settling in?"

I gripped the pike and pushed downward. Maybe I could bend it. Or maybe I could break it.

It didn't budge.

Ivan trotted closer before dismounting. He tilted his head and tapped the pike.

And suddenly, I could breathe.

"How did you do all this?" I shouted directly into his shriveled, snake-like face. "A witch couldn't have done this! Nor an elf." Was he a dark-god-controlled, turned fae? A dwarf? He *was* a little troll.

He touched my face, my shoulder, and poked at the spaces around the wound.

I winced.

He pulled back his hand. "Pain?" he said.

"I will rip your head from your horrific body. You are excrement. You are—"

"Quiet."

I could no longer speak. Ivan tapped my cheek.

"Better," he said. "Much violence in you, yes, Mr. Victorsson?" He tapped the pike. "It is good I drain it away."

I swung, fully intending to snap his vampire neck.

Ivan ducked. "Now, now." He poked at my wound again. "Why should you have a good life? Why not vampires?" He grinned a death's-head grin much like the truck behind me.

I opened my mouth, but I still could not speak.

The sigil pulsed again, and again, hot agony contracted my body.

Ivan watched the spokes progress out toward the cracks in the world. "Your enchantments lift off you when they activate," he said offhandedly. "Lift and make it easier for The One to steal your magical rib, yes?" He tapped the pike, then my cheek.

I sucked in a breath. "What did you do?" I could talk. If I knew what he did, I might be able to figure out how best to fight this, gods or not. Troll-like vampires or not.

Somewhere, out in the haze, something shrieked. Something else howled. Rustling followed.

"The call?" Ivan said. He wove his fingers into his horse's mane. "They come."

"Who, Ivan?" But I think I knew. I think I understood.

"The army," he said. "The army."

"How many?" I asked.

"How many are enough?" He clicked his tongue. "Open doors?" He waved at the haze. "Opened enough?" He waved again, then leaned close. "How many foot soldiers does a One need?"

To overrun Alfheim? To move outward from a small town and take the countryside? Not many, if they managed to immobilize the elves.

"Ivan—"

He waved his hand. My words stopped again. He stared at me through the swirling ash and mist. His snake-like features seemed to swirl right along with the ubiquitous gray, and I couldn't help but think of his seeming ability to camouflage into any situation.

With one last touch to my cheek, he released my ability to speak again. I did not open my mouth, or yell. I watched.

Ivan grasped the Percheron's reins. He vaulted onto her back—how I could not quite see through the ash—and backed her into the shadows. Then Ivan and his white horse vanished.

I was helpless. I needed to accept that, at the moment, I was as trapped as the elves. Trapped and bleeding in order to power the engine for spells a master vampire used to build a staging ground for his army.

What were they going to do once they got here? Cull the town? Enthrall the werewolves? Eat all the mundanes? Take over the businesses and set themselves up as small-town folk?

Dracula had a plan and I was helpless to stop him.

A vampire I did not know, fangs fully out and eyes hazed with red, lunged out of the ash-haze.

CHAPTER 19

The vampire swung, but missed.

A vampire, a creature with preternatural reflexes, missed grabbing my foot. I kicked him in the gut.

He was boring-looking for a vampire, with dirt blond hair, small eyes, and a round face. His clothes were also surprisingly dirty.

He must be one of the sniveling vampires. The ones easily controlled by their more powerful brethren.

"Touch me and you will be the first to die when I descend from this pike," I growled. Dracula would be the first to die, but this little rat did not know that.

He hissed and stepped back, then stuck out his tongue like a second-grade student. Then he *humphed* and walked by.

The next sigil pulse ripped through my body. I shook and groaned, but would not allow any vampire to see my pain.

Another group of vampires walked by. The leader, a raven-haired woman with porcelain skin, wore a kimono so red it gleamed in the ash-haze. Her entourage danced and skipped around her like children around a May pole.

Another vampire stopped not too far away and visibly shuddered when, out in the mist, something massive and wet rumbled out a sub-sonic scream.

Dracula's gates must have been thrown wide.

A woman appeared in front of me, close enough that she could touch my shoulder. A beautiful woman who was not there moments ago.

"Frank!" She lunged forward.

She had to be one of the vampires. How else could she have gotten into this pocket realm? Or be so lovely? "Do not touch me, vampire," I said.

She pulled back. "You have a pipe in your chest! Is it... Are you... I..." A tear appeared on her lashes and her fingers twitched as if she did not know what to do. "What did they do to you?" She reached out to touch my arm, but I pulled back.

"What kind of vampire are you?" I'd never seen one fake emotion so well.

The woman bit her lip as if I'd just crushed all her hopes and dreams. "We need to get that thing out of you! What is it? We do not have time for this." She jumped when a shriek ripped through the ash. "You don't remember me because of the concealment enchantments."

Concealments? We did *not* need complications. "What are you?"

Something I did not quite understand worked across her face. Determination? Anger? I couldn't tell. But she definitely found my questions more annoying than frightening.

"I'm your girlfriend!" she yelled. "Now shut up and listen to me!"

Girlfriend?

What kind of trick was this? I didn't have a girlfriend, and certainly not one as beautiful as this woman. "You're lying."

She *had* to be lying. She'd appeared out of nowhere.

But she did look more alive than any vampire.

"You damned well need to be more concerned about the pipe in your chest than whether or not I'm lying about being your girl-friend!" She balled her fists. "This happens every time. You don't remember but the deep parts of your brain do and you become a jackass."

Did she want to help? "You're not a magical," I said. "How did you get in here?"

"I'm a seer. I wield some magicks." She pointed at the truck. "I got Marcus Aurelius away. He's safe at my cottage. The axe didn't come back to the cottage with me. I don't know where it is."

She knew about Sal? But if she truly was who she said she was, then I would have told her everything about my life, including about Sal.

"I talked to Ed," she said. "He's back in town and has the intersection cordoned off." She looked up at me. "In the real world, your truck is abandoned and hanging open in the middle of downtown."

"It's the anchor point," I said. "This place is a waystation of sorts. A staging area."

She pointed into the ash. "The cleansing should have worked."

"It did work. They're using blood magic to counter the final cleaning phase." I tapped the pike. "This thing is built from the protection enchantments the elves gave me. It's siphoning without directly killing me. Tony said I have forty-eight hours."

She rolled over my forearms. "Your tracers are gone."

"They took those, too, to help light up the gates they're using to bring in their army."

She looked around. "Army? Of vampires? Oh, no."

What determination she had vanished. Her shoulders tightened and I swear she cringed. Defeat landed squarely on the beautiful woman who claimed to be my girlfriend. "Hey," I took her hand. I probably shouldn't have. But she had to throw off this moment or we would never escape.

She looked down at our fingers. "My name is Ellie Jones," she said. "We met two days ago. Marcus Aurelius introduced us." She looked up. "Even though it's only been two days, I'm going to stick with the girlfriend thing."

She said I was argumentative each time we met. "I'm sorry I'm a jackass when I don't remember." Something deep in the back of my mind told me that this was not the first time I'd apologized for my re-meet behavior.

Ellie touched my face. Her hand moved to my shoulder, then back to my cheek. She peered at the wound in my chest. "I didn't bring my camera because I didn't know what would happen to it in here." She looked at the wound again. "I should have brought it."

"We need to close all the portals," I said.

She looked out into the mist. "How many are there?"

I shook my head. "I don't know. The ones open right now are to places other than Alfheim. They're bringing in their army. They'll open the main portals after nightfall."

"That must be why the elves can't find them." She inhaled. "Ed told me that the elves don't even know how many portals there are but I developed the photo I took in the truck and you can see the downtown portal clear as day. Its shape. Its size. Ed said that the elves can't sense it. I think it's the same dark magic you can't see but the vampire's magicks cannot hide from a seer."

Frenzy crept into her voice. "I developed the photos I took of this place. I left them and all the others at your place. I told Ed where to find them. I'm hoping he gives them to the elves and that they pay attention." She pulled her t-shirt up over her mouth.

She pointed out into the ash again. "I saw a werewolf in the forest and I figured it was the same one who was in your truck so I followed him. I knew it was dangerous but when he's a wolf, and enthralled, he can't perceive me. I knew he'd lead me to a small, open portal where I could find you. And... and..."

The t-shirt popped off her face. She closed her mouth and inhaled again. "We need to get you off that thing."

"It's unmovable and unbreakable," I said.

She looked out into the ash. "How long is it?"

Ellie curled her hand around the pike—and screamed. She dropped to the ground holding her hand out in front of her. "I can't touch it," she wheezed. "It's like your tracers." She started panting. "We have to get you out of here. We need to close the portals before the sun sets."

There was one solution I had not yet considered. "I pulled my hatchet out of the toolbox," I said. "Dracula dropped it somewhere nearby. We could hack me off this thing."

Ellie's mouth rounded. "Dracula? *The* Dracula? How the hell did *Dracula* become part of this?"

"He was one of the corpses from which my brother was stitched."

Slowly, she stood. "And he's taken over, hasn't he?"

"Yes," I said. "Find the hatchet. I'll do it myself. You don't—"

"Oh, no you will not!" my girlfriend said. "We just met! You are not going to chop yourself into bits! We'll chop that pipe to bits! No sacrificing yourself!"

"It might be the only way," I said.

"No!" She said. "I'll figure it out. I'll make Ed get the plates to the elves so they can figure out how to find and close the gates. I'll—"

I held up my hand.

Something out in the mist squealed. A vampire laughed.

Hooves approached.

"Stay hidden," I said.

CHAPTER 20

The sigil pulsed again. I groaned, and Ellie paled, but she stayed quiet. Out in the ash, the cracks in the world brightened.

Three horses clopped out of the ash-mist. Tony's black gelding trotted up first. He stopped just outside of full visibility and reined his horse around as if confused.

Ellie stood between me and the vampire. She backed against my side and extended her arms as if shielding me.

Ivan on the white mare followed. He trotted directly to me, but he, too, seemed confused.

"They can't see me," Ellie said. "They can't see whoever is directly next to me, either."

She was hiding me? "Is this part of your concealments?" I whispered.

"Yes, but stay still. You're a lot bigger than Marcus Aurelius."

I wrapped my arm around her waist and she pressed against my side.

The horses, though, seemed to sense something.

"What have your spells done?" Tony growled at Ivan.

Ivan hissed at Tony.

They couldn't see me. I was still at the center of their spell, but they could not perceive my presence. "What kind of concealment enchantments do you carry?" I whispered.

"My mother's," Ellie responded.

Tony cocked his head and trotted closer. "The spell works," he muttered.

Hooves echoed through the ash. "Bloodyhoof," I whispered. "Dracula approaches."

Ellie nodded.

Somewhere out in the ash, someone clasped the pike. I groaned and grasped it near my heart, but the vibrations rattled my innards and for the first time, nausea took hold.

I needed to hold myself together. Ellie might not be able to hide me if I vomited.

Bloodyhoof walked closer. He snorted out brimstone. Dracula patted his neck. "There, there, lovely," he said.

He was not alone on the back of the stallion.

"An elf," Ellie breathed.

Not just any elf. "Benta the Nameless," I whispered. Dracula had stolen one of the most powerful elder elves and brought her here.

She'd lost her leather hat and her scarf was stuffed in her mouth. From the way she leaned forward, it looked as if Dracula had crossed her arms behind her back and tied them tight to her body. Her shirt had been pulled up around her eyes and made into a makeshift blindfold.

No magic flitted around her. "I think he's suppressing her magic." What were this monster and his pets capable of?

"Radu!" Dracula called. "I brought us a snack."

He pushed Benta off the horse. She fell into the ash-mist.

"Benta!" I instinctively reached out. She might be an elf, but a fall like that could kill her. She might land on her head. Break an arm or a leg—or a hand. No hands, no magic.

She yelled through the gag when she hit, but nothing seemed to have snapped. At least she was still conscious.

Ellie pressed me back. "You can't help her," she whispered.

Tony looked toward us. He frowned, then slapped at Ivan, and made him look toward us, as well. "If they get in and ruin this, I will return you to that cave, do you understand? Back to eating bats and centipedes."

Ivan hissed again. "You work the spells, then, Handsome One?"

"Why do you two fight? Enjoy your supper!" Dracula dismounted. He tweaked the pike again, and I held back a groan.

He ran his hand down the shaft until his fingers almost touched Ellie's breast. She held her breath and pressed as much against me as she could. Her pulse thumped against my skin. She shook. But Dracula did not notice us.

He leaned in, his face and fangs just inches away from her cheek, and inhaled. "Why do I smell fae?" he said, then turned toward his brother and Ivan. "Answer me!"

Ellie exhaled.

Tony's eyebrow arched and he tilted down his chin. "Perhaps you smell the stronger of the elves, brother." He dismounted and tucked his gloves into his horse's straps.

Dracula closed his eyes. He turned his face upward and he inhaled deeply just as his armor pulsed.

His hand shot out and he grabbed the pike.

Energy shot down it and directly into me. I gasped as my body imploded, as if whatever he did sucked out not just my blood, but also my muscle and bone.

This bolt pulled away my strength. I leaned against the hot metal of the truck-skull because I didn't know if I could keep myself from just hanging on the pike any longer. I didn't know if I could keep my eyes open.

Ellie turned around. She gripped my cheeks. "Stay awake," she whispered. "Please, Frank."

I gritted my teeth, but managed to nod.

Dracula walked into the mist. A scuffle followed, and more yelling. Then he reappeared dragging a bleeding, fighting Benta.

She yelled from under the gag. Her legs looked okay, but she held her left arm against her side as if the fall had done damage.

Dracula dropped her under the length of pike vanishing into the ash-mist. He rolled his shoulders and cracked his neck, then tapped the pike. "Snatching the elf gave me a sunburn." He yanked on the collar of his armor to show her the difference between his face and his neck.

I did not see a difference. Benta did not look.

Tony knelt next to Benta. "We took your precious kitty." He pointed out into the mist. "She's dead, by the way. She exploded to open one of the gates." He looked up at Ivan. "The one into Cairo, correct?"

Ivan wiggled his fingers in front of his chest much like a cartoon character. "African cat, yes?"

"Poof!" Tony splayed out his fingers. "Good-bye pussycat."

Benta hollered something through the gag.

Tony touched her cheek. "Now, now. Such assertiveness is unbecoming."

This time, she growled.

Tony sniffed at her neck. "How is it that the elves are so lovely? And you are the loveliest of the lovelies, aren't you? You're a mother goddess and a crazy cat lady all rolled up into one superbly-shaped package." He ran his hand over her chest.

A flash of light burst off Benta's skin from just over her heart. Tony howled and fell back into the ash-mist.

Benta chuckled.

Dracula grabbed her face. "Ivan tells me you're my brother's ex-girlfriend." His eyebrow arched as he looked at where he thought I should be—where I was—as if he wasn't quite not-tracking my presence. As if, somehow, Dracula's power level might outstrip even Ellie's concealments.

"How did that walking corpse bed you?" Dracula sniffed at her neck. "You're an elder elf. You are, as Radu says, 'hot.'" He stood to his full height and his head disappeared into the mists.

In front of me, Ellie stiffened. She glanced over her shoulder at me, then looked away.

"We haven't been together for a century," I whispered.

Ellie subtly nodded.

"We're not even friends. We don't talk," I said.

Ellie subtly nodded again. She didn't look at me.

"I believe you when you say you're my girlfriend."

She looked over her shoulder. A small, slight grin touched her lips.

"You will be my first bride," Dracula thundered out in the mist.

Ellie gasped. "Can he do that?"

Benta hollered again.

"She'll die before she allows him to turn her." I tightened my grip around Ellie's waist. "She'll kill herself and do her damnedest to take them with her. She's an elf."

"Benta the Nameless will now be Benta the Bride," Dracula rambled.

Ellie whispered a string of expletives. A new fear was creeping out of her, one I recognized: The rules had changed. Maybe not for me—I was huge and strong—but for the women and the mundanes. Not only was Dracula a murdering psychopath, but he was also a rapist. What he was doing with Benta moved his attacks from war to terrorism.

Benta knew it, too. Ellie understood deep in her gut.

Ivan looked as if he understood, and was not happy about it.

Dracula knelt in front of Benta. "Consent to be my bride and I will allow your people to leave," he said.

Benta snarled through the gag.

Tony chuckled.

"He's lying," I said. "She can't. She'll be his slave. She can't do this."

Ellie shook. "I can't get to her. I can't hide both of you."

Dracula sighed. "Not that it matters," he said, and bit into Benta's neck.

"Frank!" Ellie looked over her shoulder at me.

Tony pulled the gag out of Benta's mouth and tossed it to the side. She panted and tried to fight. She tried to force Dracula off, but he was too big, and she was tied and wounded.

"Do we get a bite?" Tony asked.

Dracula pulled off Benta. He wiped his mouth and looked up at his brother. "Elves are *exquisite*."

"Is turning wise?" Ivan hissed. "With elf magic?"

Tony shrugged and waved his hand up and down in front of Ivan as if pointing to evidence. "He's got a point."

Benta flopped onto her side.

Dracula poked at her with his foot. "She's still breathing."

Ellie looked at me, then at Benta. "I can't hide both of you."

If she moved away from me, they'd turn their attention this way. Maybe they'd leave Benta alone.

But Ellie couldn't move Benta because Benta couldn't see her or perceive her in any way. "What are you going to do?"

"I don't know. He can't... She can't..." Ellie hiccupped.

"Go," I said. "If there's a chance you can get her out, take it."

Ellie quickly, gently, kissed my lips.

Then Ellie Jones, the seer with the concealment enchantments, ran for Benta the Nameless.

CHAPTER 21

Ellie stepped away from me. She took one long stride and stood directly in front of Tony.

He did not notice her, but suddenly, utterly, became aware of me—as did Dracula. Ivan narrowed his squinty eyes and stepped backward into the swirling ash.

Dracula's fangs fully lengthened. Tony's descended. Both vampires' ire flamed as reddish, oily magical streaks from the sides of their eyes.

"Mr. Victorsson," Tony snarled.

Ellie looked back at me. I shook my head.

And Ellie Jones, the girlfriend I knew but did not remember knowing, dropped to her knees and huddled over the elf who was my ex.

Dracula howled like a wolf. He yowled and called and swung his thick fist at Tony's head. "How is it that you cannot control your once-witch?" he bellowed loud enough to stir the ash.

"Why would Ivan hide him!" Tony stumbled and dropped to his knees at his brother's feet. "*You* smelled fae!" he yelled. "Yet *you* did nothing!"

Dracula kicked Tony in the gut. "This from a vampire who hid as a librarian? I expected better of a Tepes." He kicked Tony again.

Ellie huddled over the unconscious Benta and did her best to stay out of the vampire fight.

Were they experiencing the same dissonance and jackass-like responses I did every time Ellie reappeared? Except with vampires, "jackass" moved into fully-raging violence.

Tony swung at Dracula and just missed Ellie's head. She yelped and ducked lower.

"Where is my snack?" Tony bellowed.

What did they remember? "The elves will destroy you," I yelled. "Can't you two see? They're ripping apart your pathetic little minds one thought at a time."

Dracula yowled again, and with two strides, was looming directly in front of me, fangs fully out and vampire rage copiously manifesting. He waved his hands at the ash. "One of the Gulf clans just came through." He inhaled sharply. "Can you not smell their ocean-sprayed indignation? I promised them your sheriff."

Out in the ash, an unseen vampire cackled.

"We will remove the pike before you fully die, my brother." Dracula gripped my face. "And we will make you watch as we reduce your body to its constituent bits."

"I find your lack of originality shocking," I said.

Dracula backhanded me across the face, then grabbed the pike to keep it from moving. A pulse lit the Dracul crest on his chest. He inhaled. And the pulse burst from his armor and into the pike.

I... moved out of my body. I displaced, or dissociated, or stopped being me. I became the misery, and the draining, and the anguish. I was the rage. I was not me.

And then I snapped back.

He'd pulled more out this time. More of my blood. More of my capability and my ability to function. He took a lot of *me*.

"We do not need you for forty-eight hours," he said.

Behind him, Tony wiped blood off his lip. He stood, keeping his eyes on Dracula the entire time, and whistled for his mount. The black Percheron trotted up. The big beast sidestepped around Ellie and Benta, and stopped at Tony's side.

The vampire mounted his horse. Dracula did not look away, or at his brother, or even acknowledge that Tony was about to leave.

Tony reined around his horse and rode off into the ash.

Dracula continued to stare at me. "I had high hopes for you." All his s-sounds slid out between his fangs as if he was a snake flicking its tongue. "I'd hoped you would understand your unique place in both The Land of the Living and The Land of the Dead."

"Go ahead," I said. "Share your hopes and dreams. We all need goals."

Dracula hissed in much the same way Ivan hissed. He rose to his full height and his head disappeared into the ash-mist. "I will take the elves' land, son of Victor." He waved his arm and the ash swirled. "I will make it my own. I will build my new castle in the New World and I will walk out onto *my* domain."

"I take it homelessness is a bit of a sore spot for you." I was too tired to spar with him. Too cold. He'd taken a lot, with that last pull. Yet I tried.

Dracula growled, but thankfully, he did not hit. He simply vanished. He disappeared into the mist as if he were the mist. Behind where he had loomed over me, Bloodyhoof tossed his head. The stallion snorted once, then pawed at the ground. He snorted a second time, then walked way.

An eerie quiet descended.

"Is he gone?" Ellie asked.

"I think so," I said. The low, sub-sonic rumble echoed again, then a groan, and the sound of shuffling. "More vampires must be passing by."

Ellie touched Benta's forehead. "She's breathing. The bleeding stopped. I wish I could activate the pull-back to my cottage. I don't know where she'd end up, but at least I'd have her out of here."

"Thank you," I said.

Ellie looked up, then back at Benta, then up at me. "She's unconscious. I can touch her without her dancing away from me the way a conscious elf would."

She hooked her hands under Benta's arms and pulled.

Ellie was going to bring the elf next to me, so she could hide us both. "Will that work?" I asked. "Stay there if it spreads the enchantments too thin."

"I have to try." Ellie tugged on Benta.

The ash spun and tightened between the women and me, and solidified into the small, horrid thing that was vampire Ivan. He raised his crooked hands, one up to his shoulder and the other to his waist, and wiggled his ugly fingers. Then he flicked out his tongue like a snake tasting the air.

"Fae?" he said.

Ellie froze. Benta groaned.

I whistled. "Ivan!" I hollered. *Snake eyes over here*, I thought.

He twisted his head to the side until his ear almost touched his shoulder. "Mr. Victorsson," he said.

I clicked my tongue at him. "I need water, you slithering reptile." Making him mad might pull his attention from whatever hints of Ellie he was picking up. "You want me to die now and close all your gates?"

Ivan stepped closer. "Where is your strength?" He poked at the wound in my chest.

"Your master sucked it out of me with that last bolt," I said. The weaker he thought me, the better.

Ivan poked at the wound. "No, no," he muttered. "Must work."

"Why?" I asked. "What do you get out of this? Those two destroyed your comfortable life in the library basement."

Ivan pulled back his fingers. "The One is my master."

"He wasn't always, was he, Ivan?" Could I reason with a vampire? Probably not. But I had to try. "You liked life in Alfheim. You took Arne's extended hand with gratitude even if Tony didn't."

He frowned.

"I'm right. You'd had your fill of being some stronger vampire's puppet. The elves offered you an alternative. *You* are why Arne let you two in. Not Tony. Tony was a hanger-on. Yet you turn on the people who helped you."

Ivan sniffed. "Scorpion. Frog." He waved his hand.

"Don't give me that Aesop's bullshit, Ivan. You're better than that."

Was he? No. He was a vampire. But maybe his soul—ghost Ivan—was. And I had no idea how much pull ghost Ivan still had with the body that was now vampire Ivan.

He flicked out his tongue again as he watched a set of shadows twirl and dance through the haze. "Vampires cannot have a good life?"

"You *had* a good life! You just returned to being a demon collared in The Land of the Dead and forced to fight for your food in the arena of the Living," I said. There was no point in sugarcoating the truth. "You're a pet like the thing you used to possess Roxy. Your life will only be as good as your owner allows."

Ivan blinked rapidly.

Perhaps I was making progress. "You pinned me here." I tapped the pike. "It's through my heart yet I still live. I still breathe. This thing is slowly sucking away my life but I'm still talking to you, Ivan. I'm still here. I'm fighting because I refuse to be someone's pet."

He tapped his foot and, once again, flicked out his tongue.

"You don't need to be his pet, either," I said.

He moved so fast I did not see him change positions until his bony hand wrapped around my neck. "Why do you stink of fae?" he snarled.

I grabbed *his* neck with my considerably larger hand. "You were a seer, weren't you?" I snarled back at him. "You were witch-blood. Did you ask to be changed? Was the witch in you getting to be too much? You couldn't handle the pain, could you?"

Ivan snapped his fangs, but I held him off.

"Weak little Ivan," I said.

Benta stirred.

"Frank!" Ellie said. "Her instincts will tell her to move away from me!" She leaned over Benta anyway.

Ivan yanked out of my grip and whipped around and sniffed at the thick air.

"Ivan!" I bellowed. "You were a fae-born seer, weren't you? A witch born of a fae and a human."

They happened more often than elf-human or kami-human witches, though they were still rare.

And more variable. Some were more fae than human. Some, more human than fae. Some fae-born witches did not descend into madness. Others burned up much faster than a half-elf.

He spun toward me. His mouth opened wider than it should—wider than a human's could—and he coughed out a guttural snarl.

Benta moaned.

"Don't move," I said. Ellie, Benta, or Ivan, it didn't matter, as long as Ivan kept his attention on me.

Benta rubbed her head with her damaged arm, then rolled over and groaned.

Ellie looked between me and Ivan, then crawled closer to Benta.

"There's…" But I couldn't tell Benta the truth. I couldn't get out that someone was trying to help her.

"Ivan, you have always made every single elf feel as if they should flee," I said.

Benta looked up at me.

"But those elves were smart enough to understand that fleeing would help no one."

Benta gripped her arm and pulled herself to kneeling, but she understood. She looked right at me and nodded.

"You told her without telling her," Ellie said.

Ivan howled. His crooked hands rose up into the air and he once again moved faster than I could perceive.

This time, he jumped toward Ellie.

He was right there, right in front of my girlfriend, sniffing at the air. Right next to a woman who had stood between me and a monster, and who was now standing between Benta and another monster who might be much worse than Dracula himself.

I knew she spoke the truth when she said she was my girlfriend. I felt it deep inside that sometime, somewhere, I'd considered her to be special to me. And that I would do anything I could to help her.

"Have you ever loved anyone, Ivan?" I yelled.

He backed up but did not turn around.

"Did you take a turning instead of sacrificing someone you loved? I think you did." I had no idea. None. Tony had threatened to send Ivan back to "that cave" but that could mean anything—a literal cave, another library, or a cubicle in an office building, for all I knew.

Maybe it was his ghost. Maybe I was a better judge of character than I thought. Maybe I had a bit of seer in me. I didn't know. But something told me that wherever and whenever that cave had been, Ivan had not been alone.

"I was too ugly until the war," I said. "I changed—everyone changed. But I think the women changed, too. I had a daughter to look after. Rose attracted women who had lost family, who needed comfort. Sally stayed the longest, but I was—am—too dead of a thing. Then Rose burned up and Benta and I found each other."

Ivan dropped his head to his shoulder. "The elder elf," he muttered.

"Yes, the elder elf, Ivan. Benta the Nameless," I said. "She's in Alfheim right now, doing her best to close the gates your master made you open because she has people she loves. People she will do anything to protect," I lied. His mind needed an excuse for her disappearance, so I gave him one.

Benta dropped down to sitting on her legs. Slowly, she picked up the rope Dracula had used to tie her arms. She held it up, then went about using it to stabilize her arm.

Ellie looked between the elf and the vampire. Even with the ash swirling in the air, I could tell she'd paled. Like me, she was running out of adrenaline.

But something about Ivan terrified her more than Dracula.

"Do elves love?" Ivan asked. "She loves only herself." He waved his hands.

Had he been living with elves when the vampires took him? The enclaves didn't take witches. I knew of only one—Rose.

But if he was a powerful seer who did not show strong, corruptible magic, they might have given him a chance.

Like, maybe, the elves here might give Ellie a chance. Or had given her one? I didn't know. I couldn't remember.

Benta frowned.

"I don't often get the chance to love someone," I said. "It's not fair to say what Benta and I had wasn't love. It was. It wasn't the kind of love that worked but to call it anything else is a slap at what I gave her, and what she gave me," I said.

Ivan stepped closer to me.

Come on, I thought. "It lasted on and off for decades. Then she got sick of the alcohol and ended it for good. It was my fault, Ivan."

He pointed a finger at me. "True?"

"I fell in love in college. Twice. I fell hard for one, you know? Head over heels the moment I saw her, so I know from personal experience that happens with me. It has before and I swear, sometimes, it happens again every morning."

I looked over his shoulder at Ellie.

She bit her lip.

"So my heart's been broken several times. I'm used to it. Am I willing to trip into love again every morning? I am. Because I understand that the love is the base. The work makes the relationship. And I think I'm ready to do the correct work."

Benta realized that I was not looking at her. Slowly, she climbed to her feet. Would she bolt? Did she understand? "We all need to do the correct work in this moment," I said.

Ivan, too, realized that I was not looking at him. "You speak to whom, Mr. Victorsson?" He looked around.

"To whom would you speak if you could, Ivan?" I asked.

He opened his mouth to answer, but a loud, deep rumble rolled through the ash. Benta swayed. Ellie covered her ears. Ivan jumped and hissed.

The pike glowed. I gasped as the wave moved into my chest—and once again, I ceased to be me. I ceased to function, breathe, live. I was nothing more than the oil of this spell, the thing it burned to power its engine.

I moved beyond the shock and electrical burning pain. Nothing got through, and nothing mattered.

I blacked out.

When I opened my eyes again, both Ellie and Benta were moving toward me. Neither was aware of the other's steps, and one had a damaged arm, but they moved in surprisingly similar ways.

Vampire Ivan inhaled. Realization dawned on his face.

He turned toward the women.

Ghost Ivan manifested between the vampire and Ellie. He moved and mirrored her movements on an uncanny level, all, I knew, to disguise her presence from the thing that had taken his body.

Ghost Ivan extended his arm and caught Benta's wrist. Shock rocked through her body and for a split second, I was sure she saw Ellie. But I did not know for sure.

Ghost Ivan looked at me. He nodded once.

And he and the women vanished.

CHAPTER 22

Vampire Ivan staggered into the pike.

Another shockwave hit my chest and all four of my heart's chambers double-contracted. The entire muscle, the entire pump, collapsed down into a ball.

I couldn't yell. I couldn't bellow or whisper. All that was left was for me to die and to become part of the ash flowing from the maw of the metal-skull behind me...

Dracula slapped my face. "Wake up!"

I wrenched back to consciousness. The pike was still in my chest. I was still kneeling on the coarse ground with my back against the truck-skull. Waves of semi-nausea, semi-pain pumped outward with each beat of my still-alive heart.

Vampire Ivan was gone.

I hadn't died. The vampires still skewered me. They still fed their spells with my blood and my soul, but they hadn't yet bled me dry.

Dracula's armor pulsed, but he didn't send it into the pike. This time, he placed his hand on the ground and sent his magic directly into the sigil's spokes. "It is almost time," he said.

Bodies writhed out there in the ash-mist. Vampires bumped and slapped at each other. Others twirled. Some cowered. Some watched with glowing eyes. Most seethed. But they were all real and they were all waiting.

"Time?" I coughed.

"Dawn closes some gates while dusk opens others." He stood to his full height and his head disappeared into the mist. "I am sure the Gulf clans will enjoy their time in Alfheim."

Out in the haze, several vampires coughed and cackled.

"Quiet!" Dracula boomed. "The elves will render most of you to wiggling meat." He frowned and clasped his hands behind his back. "Only the best of my children will survive. Those of you who do will have a place in this new world!"

His world, of course, would be a land where vampires farmed mundanes and kept elves as pets—a place my blood unleashed.

I gripped the pike, but I was weak. My fingers slid along its cold, rippled surface. I hadn't been able to pull it out when I had my strength, so why did I think I could now?

I tried again, anyway.

Dracula watched. "Still you attempt escape?" He flicked my forehead. "It's too late, my brother." He flicked me a second time. "Much, much too late."

"So you finish me? Your gates will close."

He shrugged. "Inevitable, anyway." He tapped a finger on his chin. "I could finish you off with the slow draining and keep the gates open, but I do believe watching your final death will be much more satisfying."

This one time, he spoke the truth. My arms had never felt so heavy, or my breathing. They'd sucked away enough of my life and life-force that I no longer had a path to salvation. This was my end.

That didn't mean I couldn't rip holes in Dracula's grand scheme. I could at least sow enough dissention to cause the vampires to kill their own.

"Ivan will betray you," I said. "As will Tony. Power and beauty, they are. Why would they be content to be subservient to a stitched-together corpse?" I coughed. "You are *not* that body. You are part of it.

What if one of your other personalities accidently surfaces? Even if you push it down, if they see, they will lose their fear of you."

Dracula kicked me in the gut. "Only I command this body."

The pain made sparks flicker on the edge of my vision.

He kicked again. "Only I command the demons who make us vampire."

More sparks. My throat closed up and I gulped.

And again. "*Me*," he roared.

Maybe this beating would be what finished me. Maybe he was mad enough to kill me before he finished his spells.

He pulled back his arm to hit me in the head, but he froze. His fist unclenched and he splayed his fingers.

A new pulse moved outward from the crest over his dead heart. This one was a darker, deeper red than any of the other pulses. This one, though it still glowed, looked more like dried blood than the life-blood it had before.

Was I truly dying this time? Did that pulse mean that the vampires had almost completely sucked away what remained of my soul?

"No," Dracula said. "You need to stay conscious." He dropped his hand to his side.

"Why?" I asked.

Dracula sniffed. "Because I wish to hear you beg for your life." He rubbed the tip of his nose with the back of his armored glove—which was not particularly lordly behavior.

Was he dissociating again?

More likely, my bringing up accidental dissociation was making him think about dissociating.

This, I might be able to use.

"That body's integrated personality had a worldliness about him. My *brother* seemed to have a better understanding of the world than *you*," I said.

His armor pulsed the deep red again, but this time, the spokes of the sigil stayed lit. This time, the red glow showed what walked out in the ash.

Hundreds, maybe thousands of vampires stalked out there, all waiting to rush the gate into Alfheim. All because I was Schrodinger's man—both living and dead—and instead of peering into the box to lock down my state, Dracula put a magic pike through my heart to force both states into coexistence.

The uncertainty of the universe—of *me*—had generated enough power to hold open his portals.

"So you believe your army is big enough to defeat the elves?" I nodded toward the milling vampires. "They won't follow you."

Dracula snorted.

"Do you understand how to lead modern vampires?" He'd "died" around the same time my father had made me. Dracula had not walked the Arctic into the New World. He had not found a place here among its peoples. He was an interloper, and no matter how many of them considered him The One, they would all eventually see him as an anachronism.

"Tony understands," I said. "Tony has the beauty and the charm to stabilize your new empire. He has the understanding necessary to lead."

Dracula hissed.

"When you get to be too much of a liability, he will have Ivan press that dagger into your shoulder *just right* and either take care of you for good, or turn you into something manageable."

He slid his heel back from me. Not a lot, but enough that the ash obscured his face a hint more than it had before. His fangs elongated once again.

He was angry.

The vampires might turn on each other. The elves might have a chance.

"Where is our skinny little sweetheart, anyway?" I asked. "I want to say good-bye one last time."

Dracula closed his eyes and turned his face upward as if to look toward a vampire-friendly sun. He inhaled ash into his undead body and clasped his hands behind his back. "You underestimate me, Mr. Victorsson," he said.

Dracula's armor expanded. It broke into its component parts, lifted off his body, and hovered about three inches off his skin.

Ash moved underneath. Slimy, oily magic that looked as if Dracula was using low-demons as the undergarments below his armor.

"I will not fall again," Dracula said.

The armor slammed down onto his body.

What had he just shown me? Was he insinuating that he had found a way to circumvent the dagger's lockdown on his ability to move in and out of The Land of the Dead?

"You're pinned in place," I said, hoping to goad him into more talking.

He grabbed the pike with both hands. "If you had understood what it is that you poked into my shoulder, you would have kept it for yourself." His shoulders tensed.

"I know it has a vessel of liquid embedded in the blade." Magic liquid I suspect would kill a vampire. Or at least I thought it would. Yet here Dracula stood.

He wiggled the pike and a new wave of disorientation flooded my body. Was I standing up? Lying on the ground? Still kneeling? For a split second, I couldn't tell.

Dracula pushed the pike shaft through me and deeper into the grit under the skull-truck behind me. He slammed the shaft through my heart and my soul.

The iron's rippling, blood-channeling surface tore at my insides. It shredded as it moved though my body. I ripped.

I gasped.

"I am the Lord of the Dead!" he bellowed. "How do we know?"

I stopped breathing.

He pushed again. "Answer me!"

I gulped, unable to speak.

Dracula laughed. "Your little witch-daughter sent you a weapon to kill a god!" He pushed again.

The tail of the pike manifested as a shadow in the ash. He'd pushed enough of it through my body that I could now see the end.

He let go and slapped me. "A *god*," he said as he patted his shoulder over where I'd sunk in the dagger. "I carry a piece of Odin's Gallows. I carry the waters of the Norn."

What had Rose given me?

Dracula leaned closer. "What does not kill you only makes you stronger." He stepped back into the ash. Slowly, he placed his hands on the end of the pike. "I want you to look at me," he said.

I closed my eyes.

"You will look at me as I press the pike through you, do you understand? I will first push it through your chest. Then I will twist it so—" He made a turning gesture against my cheek. "—and it will emerge from you fully charged. This pocket will be sated. This place will flourish, even if the gates slam shut."

He tapped his armor. "It will always accept me."

He *had* found a way around the lockdown—this pocket borderland. With my blood fully charging his pike, he would always have a connection. He could move in and out of here with impunity.

And from inside, he could make other gates.

Or Ivan could. I opened my eyes.

"Does Ivan know you plan to trap him here forever?" I coughed again. "Ivan!" I yelled. "Did you hear me? He won't let you leave here!"

"I am a god," he said again. "I command the vampires, Ivan included."

"Yes, I'm sure."

He pressed on the end of the pike again. "I have found a way to counter the piece of the Gallows in my shoulder. I will find a way to counter the treachery of my brothers, both you and Radu." He looked out into the ash.

His grin said exactly what his words insinuated—*because I am a god.*

He stepped deeper into the ash, and moved behind the foot of the pike. Slowly, in the shadows, he placed both hands on the knob melded to the end of the shaft.

"You will look—"

The growl of a revving motor roared through the ash. It swirled. It parted.

Dracula looked up just as the front end of the Magnus's witch-touched SUV slammed into his side.

CHAPTER 23

T he end of the pike—no more than three feet in front of me—caught the side panel of the SUV.

I instinctively pressed myself as far back against the hot metal of my once-truck as I could. Not that it would matter—I was barely breathing. I doubted I could lift a kitten. I was more corpse than man.

The end of the pike bit into the door. It gouged through the metal and hooked onto the frame between the front and rear doors. The forward momentum of the vehicle latched onto the pike's end and the engine revved higher.

A woman drove the vehicle. Not an elf—and not someone I recognized. But she'd just slammed a monster vehicle into an actual monster.

She looked down at the wheel and her hands lifted off. She must have felt the tug on the drivetrain from the pike.

The SUV—still moving fast, still roaring—pivoted around the end of the pike and sandwiched Dracula between its front and the truck-skull.

The entire structure shook. The SUV stopped literally inches from my shoulder. Literally a hand's width from taking off my arm, with

Dracula smashed between the fender and the truck only about four feet away.

His reach was long enough that he could grasp my neck once his shock wore off, but the hit seemed to have stunned him into unconsciousness.

I tried to gasp. I tried to breathe. My own shock clamped down on my throat.

"Frank!" the woman yelled. She fought back the SUV's airbag. "Stay conscious!"

I felt a distinct call not to pass out.

Sal. My axe was in the truck and she was talking to me. I slapped the SUV. "My axe," I panted.

"She's on the seat!" The woman pointed at the passenger side. "I don't know how, but I think Benta heard me after we flipped out of here." She wrestled with her seatbelt. "We landed on your deck. Sal was sitting on the lake shore."

She fiddled with her door, but it wouldn't open. "The SUV was sitting in your driveway."

The woman hit the door. "It's stuck."

"Who... are you?" I gasped.

She looked out at the ash. "How many of them are there?"

"Too many," I said.

Dracula moaned.

"I don't know how long he will stay out," I said. *Or if he will be Dracula when he wakes up*, I thought.

The woman crawled over the shift. She couldn't open the near door either; the pike had gouged it into a mess.

"My name is Ellie Jones," she said. "You don't remember me because I'm enchanted." She raised her leg to kick at the window. "Look away."

Ellie Jones kicked the glass and the remains dropped onto the pike before falling into the ash.

Dracula snarled.

Ellie pointed at the vampire. "He can't see me because of the same enchantments."

At least she was safe from the vampires.

"Can you reach Sal?" she asked.

I leaned toward the SUV. I could get my hand through the window, but not to the seat. "No," I said.

"Okay," Ellie said. She turned back toward the airbag. "Will this thing fully release?" She tugged on it. "I begged Benta to strap the axe into the front seat," she said. "I knew I could get back to you. I *knew*."

She came back for me? This woman who I didn't know?

Ellie yanked on the airbag. "We went on a date. You made a mean meat sauce. I decided you were worth getting to know." She wadded it up. "I'll tell you the rest when we're out of here."

"Okay," I said.

"Hold on."

Dracula roared. "What hidden magicks are you wielding, *Brother*?"

He pushed on the SUV. It rocked, but thankfully did not move.

"The elves consider me family," I said to the vampire. "They trust me. Your family does not trust you."

Ellie wrapped the airbag around Sal. "One good push and he'll be free," she said. "I hope he's slow to heal."

She lifted Sal through the window.

I snatched the handle and pulled my axe through the window. "Stay in there," I said to Ellie.

"Okay," she said.

The airbag dropped to the ground and I picked up a distinct cheer from Sal. "I missed you, too," I said to my axe.

Sal was pretty sure there was a fae-enchanted person nearby. Not that she could see or smell this individual, but strange things kept happening to her and she figured whoever it was wanted to help.

"You're right," I said.

She'd told Benta to put her in the SUV because she was *sure* the fae-enchanted person wanted that. "You're correct again," I said.

She came back because she could cut through the pike.

Dracula bellowed. "You called your hatchet back to you?" He slammed his fist on the SUV.

Sal huffed.

"She's not a hatchet," I said.

Ellie crawled into the back of the SUV. "If I can get close enough to you, he won't see you, either."

I nodded.

"I don't have a lot of strength left," I whispered to Sal.

I got the distinct impression that I needed to do my best.

Dracula swiped at me. "I will behead you!" he roared.

I dodged, but just barely. His fingertips grazed my ear. "Sal!" I said, and lifted her up to swing at the pike.

"Cut the pike and you die instantly," Dracula said. "Your true blood will spill and you will die."

I stopped. "Isn't that what you want? Me dead?"

He roared.

The tightness around his eyes suggested fear. He did want me dead, but he wanted me dead in a way that benefited him. I'd destroy more than his pike. I would destroy Ivan's complicated, intricate spells.

But at least I would stop Dracula, and maybe, hopefully, trap him here in his special-built borderland.

The back of the SUV squeaked, followed by the sounds of Ellie's feet hitting the gravel.

She limped around the side of the vehicle. "You'll bleed if you cut that." She pointed at the pike. "Is there another way?"

To what? Get me off the pike alive? "I don't think so," I said. "If he pushes it through me, I die. If I cut it and pull myself off, I die."

This was the end. The least I could do was end this with me.

She shook. Every one of her muscles tightened. "Damn it, Frank! You wouldn't give up on me and I'm not giving up on you!"

"You don't think I want you dead?" Dracula asked, thinking I was talking to him.

"You're a monster, but you understand resources," I said. I didn't look at Ellie, or answer her question. I wouldn't give Dracula any clues.

She picked up the airbag. "Keep him talking," she said. "I'm a seer. I

175

read the photos I took before coming back here. You survive. I *know* you survive."

Very quickly, she kissed my cheek. "Do what you need to do. Trust me to help." And just as quickly, she limped around the skull-truck.

Dracula swiped for my head again. I leaned away and he missed. "I will rain down death on every elf on this sorry planet!" He pushed at the SUV again, but the pike helped to hold it in place.

If I cut through the damned thing he would escape immediately.

"It's just you," I said. "I don't see Tony around. Or Ivan." I pointed out into the ash. "They're watching with the others right now, aren't they? Wondering if you really are the god you say you are."

Dracula snarled. He splayed his gloved hands over the hood of the SUV, but he didn't push, nor did he answer. "There will be punishments," he said in a calmer, more even-keel voice than he had ever used before.

Which meant he had now circled around mad into full-on ice-cold rage.

"That's what they want," I said. "They like it when you spank them, buddy."

He growled.

"Frank!" Ellie yelled. "Now!"

Sal echoed her yell.

I lifted the axe.

Light erupted from her blade. Brilliant, clear, white light that pushed outward with a shockwave that cleared the death-ash.

Every vampire shielded his or her eyes. Every one of them ducked —except Tony and his nightmare stallion.

And Ivan and his mare.

I slammed Sal down on the pike's shaft.

CHAPTER 24

The pike rang out like a broken, discordant bell and a second pressure wave blasted through the pocket land.

The vampires stumbled. Some fell to their knees.

The three horses of the apocalypse all neighed and pawed, but they bowed their big heads and stood strong between Tony and Ivan and the shock of Sal destroying their gate-spells.

My axe screamed. She ground into the pike's shaft and she shrieked in pain, but she kept cutting. She understood as well as I did that this needed to end, and it needed to end now.

Perhaps time slowed. Perhaps my perception sped up. But I knew each nuance of Dracula's hands as he dropped them to the hood. He readied to push. He readied to leap.

I looked down at my wound. The moment Sal sliced through the magic holding me together, I would no longer have a functioning heart. I would no longer be Schrodinger's man. I would, once again, truly be a corpse.

I just needed to get myself off the pike before it happened. I needed to add one final disruption to the spell.

Sal sliced through the pike.

The world—the pocket land—shifted. How, exactly, I could not tell, but something changed. Hopefully, for the better.

Sal fell silent, but I kept my grip on her handle. None of my blood dripped from the open pike shaft, most likely because of the angle, so at least I did not have to deal with that particular horror. But I felt it. I felt reality trying to pick a side—living or dead.

I didn't have much time before she settled on the one and only obvious choice.

I grabbed the pike and pulled myself forward.

"Stop!" Ellie reappeared.

She had my hatchet. "I saw it just before I took Benta out of here," she said. "I knew where to look."

I was still on the pike. Dracula watched me as if he thought I was frozen in indecision.

"Hold still," Ellie said, and swung the hatchet down on the pike extending from my back.

The shaft cracked and a jolt ran through my chest.

Ellie cried out and staggered back. She rubbed at her wrist holding the hatchet.

Chopping me off the pike was hurting her.

I opened my mouth to tell her to stop. This was my end; she didn't need to suffer, too. But she swung again before my words left my mouth.

A second crack opened. Another jolt fired through my chest.

The pike broke.

I fell onto my side. I simply dropped out of Dracula's sight and into the swirling ash-mist around my knees and feet.

He roared and pushed on the SUV. It skidded away.

The hatchet landed on the ground next to me, as did Ellie Jones. She wheezed, and looked up toward the now-free Dracula. "He can't perceive you as long as I'm close."

"Okay," I whispered.

She touched my back and my chest, but not the remnant of the pike still in my chest. "You're alive," she said.

I looked down. I was. "How?" No blood spilled.

"I think it's because the pike was built out of your... protection spells." She rolled over and clutched her stomach. "I think they're still... doing their job."

Sal agreed.

"So I have a magical pipe through my chest that refuses to let me die?"

She also looked pale. Not just the level of pale one would expect inside the vampire's borderland, but fully, ghostly pale.

Dracula howled and turned in a circle. "What has happened to my spell?" he yelled. "Where is Victorsson?"

He couldn't see me. "You're doing that?" I asked.

"Yes," she said.

"I think I love you, Ellie Jones," I said, which was a truly odd thing to say, considering.

She leaned her head against my shoulder. "You are head over heels in love with me, Frank Victorsson. It's obvious."

"I'm glad one of us has it figured out," I said. "You saved me."

Ellie moaned. "Not yet."

Dracula pushed the SUV again. He snagged the now-cut end of the pike and yanked it upward.

Ellie and I rolled out of his way.

"He's trying to salvage what he can," I said.

I curled my arm around her waist and pulled her as close to my side as I could.

The ash had settled, but the gloom persisted. The horde of vampires backed away from the thrashing Dracula. And just on the edge of the shadows, Magnus's three possessed horses snorted and pawed.

I looked down. The sigil lines had vanished. Out in the distance, the gates had vanished, as well.

We were trapped in here with an army of vampires.

Unless...

"You said that you came back, correct?"

"Yes," Ellie answered.

"How?"

"Your truck. In real life, it's the brightest, most obvious of the gates."

"What did you do?"

She looked up at my face. "I drove the SUV at it."

"Do the elves know you're here?"

She shook her head. "They can't sense me any better than the vampires." She held tightly to my waist. "I tried, Frank. I left evidence. I'm hoping Ed understands."

"But you *drove an SUV* though it." I said. "An SUV is a lot bigger than me."

She leaned against my side. "Do you think they saw the car?"

"I'm hoping." Yes, I really was in love with this woman.

Dracula roared. Tony and Ivan watched from behind the horses. The horde became an indistinguishable haze in the shadows. And cutting me off the pike had drained Sal. I held her up. "She's unconscious. What do we do?"

"My enchantments will pull me home." Ellie pressed herself against my side. "You're the biggest person, pet, or object I've ever tried to move."

She seemed unsure. "If I don't go, get to Ed. Do what you can, okay?" I said.

"I will."

"How long?" I asked.

She frowned. "Dusk had settled when I drove through. It shouldn't be—"

A flash of *dark* pulsed out from behind the horses. Where Sal burst out a bright flash that pushed back the dark magic, this burst pushed back her light.

Tony stepped between the two Percherons.

Ivan looked out from behind his back.

Ghost Ivan appeared between us and Tony and vampire Ivan. A ghost of a man who might once have been a witch like my dead daughter, Rose. Ivan, who instead of burning up, was burned away by a demon who consumed his soul.

He bowed his head.

Then ghost Ivan, the entity who had been helping me from the moment this first started, sucked down to a small ball of energy that settled onto vampire Ivan's outstretched palm.

"We know you are still here, Mr. Victorsson," Tony said. "Come out or we send Ivan's immortal soul into the deepest, most tormenting pits of Hell itself." He looked at vampire Ivan. "And then we open that pit onto the world."

CHAPTER 25

One last pull and Dracula freed his pike from the pocket land's floor. He tossed it a few times, each time moving his hand along the shaft as he tested for the weapon's new center of gravity. He thrust it upward, then twirled it around himself like an eight-foot-long baton.

He might not sense us, but he could still hit us. I pulled Ellie closer to the skull-truck. It wouldn't offer a lot of protection, but a random swing was less likely to hit if we were near the vehicles.

"So Ivan's caught his wayward soul, has he?" Dracula chuckled and swung the pike again. "Give it to me." He held out his hand and wiggled his fingers.

"*My* soul," vampire Ivan hissed. He closed his fingers around the little ball of energy and pulled it close to his chest.

"You would deny The One his rightful spoils?" Dracula roared. "I am a god!"

"I think Tony's plan backfired," Ellie said.

Could we be that lucky? "I tried to get them to turn on each other the entire time they had that stick in my chest."

"Looks like you succeeded."

Vampire Ivan ducked behind his horse. "It's mine!" he squeaked.

182

Tony slapped Ivan, who hissed like a snake.

Dracula slammed the point-end of his pike into the ground yet again. The remaining chunk no longer towered into the ash, but ended in a cracked, jagged point next to his ear. "You two allowed Victorsson to escape!" He dove at Tony.

The three vampires hit at each other and rolled into the shadows.

I couldn't let vampire Ivan feed on his immortal soul. I couldn't allow the ghost who had helped me to end up in eternal torment as food for demons.

Because "the pit" wasn't fire. Nor was it ice. The pits were the only places in The Land of the Dead where entropy did not reign supreme —it was the one place where the vectors, whirlpools, and cyclones fought against the entropy. The places that made demons both low and high—and also sometimes created angels.

It wasn't just about doing good by ghost Ivan, either. Who knew what would come out of a pit fed by that much power?

"We have to get Ivan's soul," I said.

Ellie had saved me. We'd closed the gates into this pocket land. Now we just needed to make sure the vampires never left—or unleashed something worse than themselves.

Dracula and Tony rolled toward the horses. The Percherons continued to paw and snort magical fire, but Bloodyhoof raised his head and twisted his ears toward the skull-truck as if listening.

Out in the shadows the unsure, unseen horde seethed.

And Ivan stared at the ball of energy on his palm.

"Stay where you're safe from his pike," I said, and stepped away from Ellie.

"Frank!" She reached for me.

Every bit of living being in my semi-dead body yelled to stay next to Ellie. Every bit of me wanted to never again let her go, but I had to get Ivan's soul.

And I had to end this one way or another.

"Stay put," I said, and stepped out of her protective shadow.

Tony landed a punch before Dracula threw him off.

"Do you all still believe Dracula is The One?" I yelled at the horde. "He and his brother fight like toddlers!"

Dracula jumped up to a squat. He glared at me and held up his hand to indicate to Tony that he wished to suspend their squabble.

Then he picked up his pike.

"Frank!" Ellie curled her arms around my waist and tried to move me to the side. I rolled with her, trusting her instincts, and the pike flew through where my chest had been.

"I am *not* staying put!" she said. "If I'm close, you can cloak if you need to."

Never in my life had I fought with someone who could make me appear and disappear from an opponent's senses.

Perhaps I needed to learn.

Dracula hollered and slapped the ground. "He was here!" He slapped it again. "Is he moving in and out? Does he have access to a gate I do not see?"

The third time he slapped the ground, the sigil lines lit up.

The gates were closed, but something swirled around the ruins of the SUV. Something familiar.

Fireflies.

Had Ellie brought with her some of the enchanted ash—the soot the vampires used on the *other* side to open the gates? The swirling fireflies that had cracked space and time? A few of them must have backwashed into the pocket land when she drove through at high speed.

Dracula couldn't see them, nor could Tony. Ivan, perhaps. Ellie, maybe, but she'd said something about using photos as her seer stone.

Just me and my ability to see magic.

I hadn't noticed them before because the ash here was too thick. But Sal had cleared away most of it and the dust clearly flickered around the SUV.

Ellie coughed. She bent over and moaned. "Frank." She grabbed for my hand. "The pull."

I could pick her up and move with her, or I could stay and fight. I could save the woman I loved—and I was pretty sure I was in love with her, enchanted or not—or I could make sure these vampires never hurt anyone ever again.

She coughed again, and dropped to her knees. "It's not working. I'm not leaving." She cried out. "Stop, stop, stop!" She rolled onto her side.

I dropped to my knees next to her. "Your enchantment spells can't move you out of here?" I looked around. "Because the gates are closed?"

She nodded, but didn't respond.

Would it kill her? I needed to get her out of here.

I looked back at the prancing vampires. I needed to get her out without letting them out—or leaving them with an energy reservoir that was Ivan's soul.

"Sal?" I said. "Please wake up."

Sal's handle vibrated against my palm, and the violet-blue of the magical bands around her handle glistened. I got a distinct impression of grogginess.

"Do you think you can pull the enchanted ash together and open enough of a portal to get Ellie out of here?"

She considered killing vampires to be more important.

"Can you do both?" I asked.

She couldn't. Either she enticed a small portal, or she killed vampires and took back Ivan's soul.

"Get Ellie out of here." *You and I will stay*, I thought. I would kill all the vamps with my bare hands.

Sal reminded me that I still had a pipe in my chest.

I was also still weak. But I wouldn't go down without a fight. And Ellie would be safe.

Sal flashed. The fairy-light ash pulled together, and—

Dracula covered the twenty or so feet between us faster than I could lift Sal to shield his change. He slammed into me at a full run.

I held my ground as best I could, but the hit felt like a truck collision. Another hit like that and I'd likely pass out.

We stumbled into the still-burning skull-truck. Dracula swung to punch. I blocked with Sal and she fired a bolt of light magic into his armor. Not a major bolt—she was as weak as I was—but enough to get him to fall away.

The enchanted ash swirled and swooped, but not as if Sal's attempt to charm it into cooperating worked. It swirled more like drunken pixies.

No portal would open. I couldn't get Ellie out of here. And Dracula was still close enough to do damage—and much closer to the writhing Ellie than I liked.

By the horses, Ivan leaned over his soul and muttered words I did not understand. Tony watched with keen eyes my fight with Dracula. He did not move to interfere.

"Your brother is scheming to destroy you." I pointed at Tony.

"His name is Radu." Dracula wiped his mouth on the back of his armor's glove. "And he understands who the god is here."

Tony minded the Percherons, but Bloodyhoof tossed his head and sidestepped toward the SUV. Ellie coughed. Dracula seemed too caught up in his own narcissism to notice anything or anyone but me.

Vampire Ivan looked up. He opened his palm again, and held out his hand.

His soul had changed—no, he'd trapped it. It still burned bright white, but now from inside a cage of shadowed lines.

It floated off his palm.

The lines curled and uncurled—and formed the same pattern as the sigil on the ground.

I wasn't the only one working on opening a new gate.

Tony grinned his handsome vampire grin.

They would invade Alfheim without Dracula. They knew the town —and many of the elves. They would trap us all here—me, Sal, Ellie, all the idiot vampires who heeded Dracula's call, Dracula himself— and take with them the knowledge they had promised to their One. They would use it solely for their own benefit.

Of course they would. Every single vampire in the horde would do exactly the same thing if they had the opportunity, power, and intelligence. As would have Dracula, if he wasn't so adoration-needy.

So every bit of my prodding, every one of my assertions that Tony and Ivan would turn on Dracula, had been correct.

I was right, but it would still likely get Ellie and me killed—and still destroy Alfheim.

"We have one chance here, Sal," I said. Once chance to free Ivan's soul, and to close the final gate, and to keep Alfheim safe. It would likely lock us in here, but I didn't see any other way.

I'd take an eternity in a pocket borderland to save the world from a horde of vampires.

Sal agreed.

Maybe the release of energy would open the pocket land enough for Ellie's enchantments to pull her free. Maybe not. I couldn't know for sure. But I had to try. "I'm sorry, Ellie," I said.

Confusion blanketed Dracula's face.

My throwing arm isn't excellent. Even after two centuries, my brain still does not quite understand the piecemeal body it drives. But I did practice, and I wasn't bad.

I threw Sal at the ball of energy that was Ivan's soul.

The Percherons bolted. One knocked Tony on his ass. The mare jumped toward Bloodyhoof as if the stallion would protect her.

Ivan, too, fell away from the ball of energy.

Sal twirled vertically in the air at a true, perfectly perpendicular angle to the ground. She flew straight, axe-head over axe-handle, and cut through the pulsing shadow sigil caging Ivan's soul.

The cage ruptured and Sal carried ghost Ivan deeper into the gloom—and into the vampire horde. I'd have another fight on my hands getting her back.

Vampire Ivan shrieked. Tony clawed at the ground. Dracula stared like a dumbfounded child.

And Ellie—she was still in a ball on the ground next to the skull-truck. Still moaning. Still here, but the air around her shimmered.

The ash fireflies were congregating around her body as if drawn like moths to her enchantments.

I scrambled toward her. "Ellie?" I said.

Dracula jumped up to a squat again. "Where is he?" He slapped the ground and reached for his pike.

Tony had other plans. Tony ran for it first.

Dracula tripped him and he skidded through the dust. "You attempt to take my pike? Will you also attempt to steal my low-demons?" His under-armor writhed out from below his Dracul breastplate. "You will not escape this place, Radu! Not after your pathetic showing of your true nature."

Tony dodged a swing. "You are not The One," he said. "I let my hope that my brother would be what we needed cloud the obvious. You are *not* The One."

Dracula pushed him away from the pike. "I carry part of Odin's gallows!"

Tony lifted both his hands over his head in a double-fisted punch and brought them down on the broken dagger was embedded in his shoulder and under Dracula's armor.

Or not Dracula. The mighty vampire body built by my father. Dracula was only a part of that monster.

Dracula gulped. He covered the spot with his hand and staggered backward. "I will kill you for that!"

Ellie groaned—and the fireflies formed a new sigil over her body.

A familiar sigil.

I dropped over her body just as a rip opened in the fabric of the pocket universe—and a bow-wielding elf in full body armor jumped through.

CHAPTER 26

E llie didn't vanish. She should have vanished, should have been pulled through and to safety, yet she still lay unconscious under the sigil.

I checked her pulse. She breathed, but she didn't move.

I could carry her out. I should carry her out, but then the elf firing vampire-killing arrows would be here alone.

The horde screamed. Tony ducked behind the SUV and the skull-truck. Dracula dodged and wove between the arrows as he tried to reach his pike.

In front of me, Magnus Freyrsson fired arrows and bellowed threats. Magnus, Alfheim's most lovable elf, stood like an imperial war god between Ellie and me, and a massing army of angry vampires.

I'd only once before seen an elf in full body armor. Magnus's, like all things elven, reflected his connections to the natural world, and echoed natural leaf and water shapes. It gleamed, but more with magic than with metal. The overlapping layers of his chest coverings were more supple than any metal, and were more like elven ballistic wear than any suit of Medieval plate armor.

His semi-conical helmet both distorted the visual lines of his head and served as a beacon of magical power.

Light streamed off him—real, bright light, as well as blinding magical energy.

This was Magnus Freyrsson, elder elf, and he raged.

"Blodughofi!" he yelled. "Come, boy!"

Out in the ash, Bloodyhoof whinnied.

"Lucky! Comet! Come!"

The two Percherons also whinnied.

"You dare take my mount?" Dracula called out. He stood to his full height and puffed out his chest as if he thought taking on an enraged elder elf was a good idea.

Magnus sniffed. "Ask yourself, you giant bombastic roll of vampire sushi, why *I* am the elf who stepped into your hidey-hole. Why is it not our King? Our Queen? Benta, whom you *dare* harm? Or our army? Why *me*?"

His next arrow took off Dracula's ear. Literally ripped it off the side of his head.

Dracula screeched.

"You stole *my horses*!" Magnus pointed a gloved hand and sneered at the vampire. "I will slaughter all of you," he said, slowly and with distinct diction.

Never in my life had I ever seen an elf radiate back to a vampire its own malevolence. Never had I seen an elf mimic mannerisms or body language of a foe so well. But Magnus was once a popular and sought-after actor.

Another of Magnus's arrows ripped by Dracula's head. The giant dodged this time, and I doubted Magnus would hit him again.

Dracula stepped back into the ash.

Magnus sniffed again and rained more arrows into the vampire horde. "How is it that you pathetic, ugly, sniveling little sewage-dwellers thought that I would allow you to *steal my horses*!" he bellowed.

I hoped this was an act. A loud, theatrical act designed to terrorize the terror-inducing, or Magnus was more than he let on.

I stepped away from Ellie. "Magnus!" I called.

"Frank." He pointed over his shoulder at the rip. "Where the hell have you been hiding? We close this pocket for good."

Out in the ash, vampires wailed.

"Where are my horses?" Magnus yelled. More arrows rained into the vampires. "I *hate* vampires. You idiots ruined a good thing! You two whiny miscreants could still be enjoying your library life but no, you had to mess it up. You had to go crawling back into the dark."

Lucky and Comet—the Percherons—galloped out of the ash and straight for Magnus. They stopped before their owner, both with their hellfire-infected heads low.

Magnus flipped his bow over his shoulder. His arms bent and his elegant, dexterous fingers danced through the air.

A sigil appeared between the horses and the rip.

"Go on," he said to the horses. "This will help." He stepped to the side.

The two horses snorted. The gelding wagged his head. Then both horses jumped through the sigil and back into the real world.

"Blodughofi!" Magnus yelled. "Let's go!"

I needed to get Ellie out of here, and get Sal and Ivan's soul. Then they could close up this place for good.

"Magnus. I need to fetch Sal." I pointed into the horde. "Otherwise they'll open the gates again."

He looked me over. "You have a pipe in your chest, Mr. Victorsson," he said. "How are you walking?"

I looked down at the wound. "Dracula built it out of my protection spells."

Magnus sniffed again. "He built it *out of your protection spells?*" He waved his hand over the open end of the pipe sticking out of my chest. "Vampires?" He scoffed.

"Yes," I said.

"More the reason to trap them here." He whistled for his stallion once more. "I will maim every one of you *disgusting* bloodsuckers for harming the jotunn of Alfheim!" he roared. "And then I will rip you into *pieces* for harming my *horses!*"

191

"Magnus, I need you to…" I couldn't finish my sentence. I couldn't ask him to take Ellie through the rip.

Damn it, I thought. "Can you hold them off long enough for me to get Sal?"

Magnus shouldered his bow again. "There is fae magic here," he said.

He sensed Ellie. "Yes," I said. "Fae magic I need to deal with."

"Fine," Magnus said. "We leave the moment my stallion returns to me."

"Okay, okay," I said.

He looked me over again, then pointed at the wound. "If you go through, will that kill you?"

I looked down at it. "Probably." What else could I say? I didn't know.

He frowned. "I will exit first. Arne, Dag, and Benta hold the rip on the other side. I will tell them you will need immediate tending."

Thing was, I would be carrying Ellie and they wouldn't know when I came through.

"How far away is Salvation?" Magnus asked.

Through the rip, I thought, then it dawned on me who he meant.

My axe could have told me her full name.

Out in the ash, a faint call told me to stop whining and to come pick her up before Magnus closed the rip.

"I hear her, Mr. Victorsson." Magnus held up his hands as if to draw out a new sigil. "Go save your axe."

I looked down at Ellie. "Be careful where you step."

Magnus looked down. He frowned. But he nodded.

I dragged myself into the ash-mist. Dracula was out here, as were Ivan and Bloodyhoof. And perhaps Tony, who was much more likely than Dracula to command the horde.

Keep calling, I thought. A talking axe would be easier to find than a silent one. *Please tell me you have Ivan's soul.*

A muffled feeling of *over here* came from just ahead and a little to the left. I stumbled forward.

I saw Sal's light shimmer in the shadowed gloom. She looked

whole and unbroken, so at least vampire Ivan's magic hadn't cracked her, but I couldn't tell if she'd freed Ivan's soul, or sucked it in, or was protecting it some other way.

I reached for my axe.

Vampire Ivan manifested out of the ash directly behind Sal. He wasn't hovering, or slinking, or attempting to snatch. He simply sat next to her cross-legged like a monk.

"Mr. Victorsson," he hissed.

When I attempted to grab Sal's handle, he slapped away my hand. "A boon?" he said.

I snagged her handle anyway.

Ivan wrapped his spiny fingers around my forearm.

He was serious about his boon. "From you to me or me to you, Ivan?" I answered.

He looked up. "A cage is always a cage, Mr. Victorsson, no matter how well lined with books."

I frowned. "Ivan, I…" What could I say to that? To a vampire?

Ivan let go of my arm. "Expressiveness speaks volumes." He touched his nose. "Boon?"

"Fine," I said.

He hovered his hand over Sal. "Many effects." He snatched back his fingers. "This close. Connections reestablished."

Ivan slapped my forehead. "Remember," he said, and vanished.

Nothing magical happened. No lights or new pain, or that shifting feeling that comes with a spell. Nothing but a vampire slapping me on the head and then vanishing.

I picked up Sal. "What did he do?" I asked.

She had no idea, though she did echo my feeling that whatever it was, it wasn't magical.

And she had his soul. Vampire Ivan had followed them into the gloom and sat with her and himself and she was pretty sure he'd been affected.

He hadn't attacked me. "Seems likely," I said.

Her blade shimmered extra bright, but I didn't feel any extra magic. "So ghost Ivan is along for the ride?"

An affirmative washed from the axe as I swung her up to my shoulder.

Something hit me from behind—and latched on. A slimy, wing-like thing slapped against my shoulders. The creature shrieked and snapped and dug its talons and teeth into my flesh.

My entire attention shifted to the horror humping my shoulders. "Get off!" I yelled, and slapped at my upper back.

I missed the straight jab into my nose.

Dracula had reattached his ear. Magnus's arrows must have carried some sort of dissolution magic because this time, it continued to look bloody and torn, unlike when Jax ripped it off.

I swear the bat-thing on my back snickered.

I swung Sal. Dracula whipped around his pike and danced out of the way.

The next hit came to the back of my knees. I dropped to the grit.

Dracula kicked me in the lower back. "You think this is done, do you?"

His foot made contact with the pipe in my chest. I gasped and fell backward onto the bat-thing.

It huffed and squealed, and bit harder. I howled, but landing on it did damage. I arched my back to keep the pipe end off the ground, lifted my shoulders, and and rounded my back opposite the arch.

I smacked down on the ground again.

The bat-thing burst like a sack of jelly.

I couldn't retch no matter how disgusting the ex-thing on my back was. Vomiting wouldn't get me out of this. Or Sal. Or Ellie.

Dracula laughed. "I'm going to open a real hole in your chest," he snarled as he lifted the pike to jab me through my real heart.

He must have heard the galloping first because he looked up.

Bloodyhoof knocked him on his ass. The huge horse pawed and tossed his head. His eyes, though still red, no longer glowed, and he no longer snorted hellfire.

Whatever magicks Magnus wielded to un-possess his horses seemed to extend out here to Bloodyhoof.

Dracula slapped the ground. "I will skin you, you ungrateful—"

Bloodyhoof reared up. And Bloodyhoof, Magnus's magnificent, elven-bred stallion, dropped a front hoof onto Dracula's shoulder.

The remains of the dagger broke with such force I heard it crack. The vessel of Norn's water shattered. The wood splintered.

The personalities inhabiting the vampire body stitched together by my father fully dissociated.

My "brother" gasped—and whatever manifested was more like me the moment I awoke than like Brother or Dracula.

He howled. He scratched at the dirt. Then he staggered to his feet and ran into the ash.

"Thank you," I said to the stallion.

Was my brother gone for good? Only if we closed off this pocket.

His pike lay on the ground a few feet away. "Take it with us or leave it here?" I asked Sal.

She had no idea, but clearly did not want to be anywhere near it.

"Leave it here, it is," I said.

Magnus called Bloodyhoof again. The stallion looked up and whinnied his answer.

I stood. I wouldn't try to get on his back without a saddle, not in my condition, but I patted his neck. "We must be careful of the vampires." The horde was inching forward, and who knew if my brother-monster would attack again.

Sal agreed.

Bloodyhoof tossed his head again.

"We're coming!" I yelled. "Stay near," I said to the horse as I led him toward the elf.

The moment Magnus saw Bloodyhoof, he brightened and extended his cleansing sigil. "Damned vampires," he yelled.

The stallion trotted up. Magnus rubbed his snout. "It'll be fine, boy," he said, and sent his horse through the rip. "Come, Mr. Victorsson."

I held out Sal. "The moment you see me, tell them to seal the rip, then attend to my wound."

Magnus frowned, but took the axe.

She wasn't happy.

"I can't carry both of you," I said to Sal.

Magnus looked confused. "Fae magic?" he asked.

"Yes," I said. "No matter what you perceive, I will be coming through after you."

"All right," he said.

"Go." I waved him toward the rip and dropped to my knees next to Ellie.

She moaned.

"I'm going to pick you up," I said.

Magnus leaped over us and through the rip.

"You're wounded," she whispered.

I scooped her up. "It's almost over—"

Someone knocked us through the hole into the real world.

CHAPTER 27

I staggered into Alfheim's downtown intersection, Ellie in my arms and a pipe still in my chest.

I dropped her. I tried not to. I tried to break her fall, but she fell out of my arms onto the pavement just as whatever hit me in the back rolled to the side.

Tony. He rolled into a crouch and snarled.

He still wore his Dracul armor, and it still seethed as much as he did.

The first bolt of elven magic knocked him on his side. The second picked him up and slammed him ten feet up the side of the gallery building's wall.

The elves had him. I didn't need to fight. I...

I dropped to my knees. Ellie groaned but was alive and conscious. She reached out, but pulled back the moment she noticed the elves running toward me.

They were all in full elven armor. Arne and Dag, who both wove spells around the rip. Benta, who held Sal. Magnus and the seven other elves who blasted Tony.

Benta dropped to her knees and set Sal on the ground. "Hold still." She wove a sigil over the wound.

I had no real, physical wound. No broken bones or blood escaping. The pike's shaft still stuck out of my chest, but it shimmered now, and looked more like a woven spell than anything real or metal. "Can you... see it?" I panted.

"I know where it is," Benta said. "I saw it in the pocket realm."

My heart... slammed. It threw itself against my breastbone because it refused to stop. It refused to give up.

A few feet away, Ellie sat up. "Frank. Hold on," she said.

I reached out to her.

"I can't," she said. "I'll interfere."

Benta looked down at my fingers, then over her shoulder. "Right," she said. "They're Arne's spells."

She thought I was pointing at the other elves.

"Arne!" she yelled. "You put his protection spells in place! You need to take them off!"

My heart slammed again.

"Now, Arne Odinsson!" Benta yelled.

By the building, Magnus and the other elves blasted Tony.

He vanished. Literally disappeared out from under the magical blasts holding him against the wall. Did they destroy him? Did he pull a vampire and glamour his way out of the fight? I had no idea.

Arne knelt next to Benta. "It's through his heart?"

She pointed. "Here."

He placed his hands on my chest. "I feel it." He nodded over my shoulder. "Hands here," he said to Benta, and placed her palms directly over the bit of spell-pipe in my chest. "I need to push it out from the back."

"Okay," she said.

"Unweave it as it comes out," Arne said.

"Yes," she said.

My heart slammed again.

Arne moved behind me. "This will hurt, son," he said, and smashed his fists against my spine.

That hit would have broken the back of a mundane man. I fell forward onto Benta.

198

She kept her hands on my chest and she unwove the spell. Freed magic curled out from between us like a cloud of shimmering, rainbow-filled pixie-ash.

All the stolen safety of what had once been my protection spells undid. All the crashing of power against my heart stopped. All the manipulations of the spaces in and around my body ceased. Every sense of barriers between me and the unforgiving world vanished.

I was... naked. I'd spent so much time inside armor provided by the elves that I'd forgotten what breathing unfiltered air felt like.

And I... I was physically whole. I was alive with a living heart and no pike in my chest.

It felt good. Frightening and new, but good.

I almost kissed Benta to say thank you. Almost. But there was another who... I rolled off Benta and looked around. Magic filled the intersection and the entire area glowed with a bright, beautiful, living light. Magnus and the other elves had dealt with Tony. The rip was sealed. And a cruiser approached, lights on and sirens whooping, which I assumed was driven by Ed.

It was over, except I was sure I was supposed to remember something. Or someone.

Benta removed her helmet, as did Arne.

"Ed found photographic plates of their portal magic on your kitchen table," Arne said. "He said they fell out of Rose's notebook."

Rose gave us pictures of what we needed to fight?

Arne unbuckled his armor. "She was your daughter, Frank. Even when the insanity took her, she was still a good person." He squeezed my shoulder.

Something about the whole thing wasn't right.

"The cleansing spells did their job and concentrated the enchanted ash," Benta said. "We caught Mark Ellis near one of the smaller gates and released him from the low-demons. That's how Magnus knew he could save his horses." She pointed over at the three now-calm show horses. "We couldn't close any of the portals because they had you."

She, too, unbuckled her armor, but favored her sprained arm. "I let Dracula take me so I could recon the pocket realm."

"She came back with the axe," Arne said.

"Sal told us we needed to toss the SUV at you." Though she frowned as if her recollections didn't quite line up with the evidence.

She touched my chest. "I'm glad you're okay."

Dag removed her helmet as she walked over. She did not look happy. "No more vampires in Alfheim, husband."

Arne scowled but he did not answer. Benta sighed.

Had Arne been wrong to allow Tony and Ivan in seventy years ago? Maybe. I didn't know, and right now, I didn't want to take on that fight.

Arne squeezed my shoulder again. "It's done, son. Go home. Sleep. Come to The Hall tomorrow and we will discuss the meaning of all this." He waved his hand at the town, then walked away to talk to Ed.

"Yes," I said. "In the morning." I patted my chest. No real damage. But my arms continued to feel heavy. Laying my head on the asphalt and taking a nice, long nap seemed a viable alternative.

So Arne was correct; I needed rest. We all needed rest.

Sal agreed. Morning would be best.

I picked up my axe. "Where's Ivan's soul?" I asked.

He was free and safe.

"What does that mean?" More spirit vagaries, but this time not from the spirit himself.

Sal thought for a moment, then the sense of *free* I got from her changed to *actualized* or perhaps *purposeful*.

"That makes even less sense, Sal," I said.

Benta smiled. "I don't think we will ever understand." She put her hand on my chest again. "I want to make sure you're okay."

I understood perfectly well the look on her lovely face. I understood the set of her fingers and the delicate dance of her touch.

More vagaries danced along the margins of my mind. Something about these last few days reminded me of my own loneliness. I might be used to it, but that didn't mean I liked it. And the touch of a kind woman went a long way to calm at least some of those choppy waters.

"So you forgive me for Roxy?" I had to ask, anyway.

"You were not at fault." She looked away. "Some of the things you said while we were in the vampire's ash realm made me remember how good you really are, Frank."

I, too, looked away. I wasn't quite sure I remembered the same moments she did, but that really wasn't important.

Ed waved. The elves seemed to have everything under control.

Benta took my hand. "Come on. I'll take you home."

REAL FIREFLIES DANCED over the lake. Frogs chirped in the evening air. Benta took the glass of wine I offered and patted the swing's seat.

"Sit down," she said.

We'd stopped at her place before coming back to mine so she could change out of her armor. I'd waited out front listening to her cats roar. She'd come out with the wine and a bag over her shoulder.

I didn't argue. Having company tonight seemed like a good idea.

The swing creaked when I sat.

Benta watched me slowly descend. "I have missed you." She sipped her wine.

Moonlight reflected off the Carlson ruins and I wondered about my own reflections. "I've changed a lot since we were together." I sipped from my own glass.

Benta set hers on the deck. "I hope so." Her fingers worked across my shoulder to my neck. "Are you going to have Arne or Dag replace the protection spells and the tracers?"

I looked down at my arms. "I don't know." Part of me whispered that this was the type of freedom that might hurt more than help, but it did mean I could breathe. Another part liked that little bit of armor the spells had provided, but yet another said that armor also caused problems.

Not just vampire problems, either. "Did they... tingle... when you touched them?" I don't know why I asked. The question didn't make a lot of sense.

Benta shook her head. "I'm an elf," she said, as if her elfhood explained everything.

"I'm going to need to look for my dog in the morning," I said. He'd run off again, but something told me that he was fine.

Again, I didn't know why. Maybe because we were all just fine, now that the vampires were gone.

Benta leaned against my shoulder. "I think you should get a cat."

Of course she did. "Cleaning up Marcus Aurelius's hair is bad enough. I don't know if I want a selfish ball of fluff around, too."

She chuckled.

"I think you should call yourself Bastetsdottir."

Her chuckle turned into a laugh, and she crawled onto my lap. "I really did miss you."

Part of me wondered if she truly did forgive me for Roxy, and for our break-up a century ago, and for the many and myriad pokes we'd always taken at each other. There were reasons we didn't talk.

But she was Benta the Nameless and she had the kind of feline grace and loveliness that acted like a drug. Benta was easy to touch and easy to be with, because Benta was living, breathing art.

Art that, on the surface, soothed.

I ran my hands over her hips. "We shouldn't do this," I said.

She kissed my chin and my jaw. "Someone needs to keep an eye on you tonight."

"Hmmm…" I said. She was probably right.

I WAS ALONE in my bed when I woke up. No Benta. No Marcus Aurelius licking my nose, either. Just me and the sound of someone brewing coffee in my kitchen.

Benta never liked being in my bed in the morning. She wanted to give me the space I needed to warm up, she liked to say.

I guessed some things never changed.

The sun streamed in through the window, but at a low enough angle it couldn't be too late. She had, at least, allowed me to sleep off the residue of the vampire enchantments.

My chest didn't look any worse for wear. No new scars or sore patches. My morning stiffness didn't feel any worse than usual. And Benta did provide my body with her perfect elven touches.

Perhaps I did manage to come though my pike-through-the-chest ordeal okay. So why did I still feel... distraught? Upset? Alone? I didn't know.

I pulled on my boxers and walked out into the kitchen.

Benta, topless, spectacular, and wearing only her white cotton panties, leaned against my countertop. She propped her elbows on the elevated granite and thrust out her exceptional breasts. "Good morning, gorgeous."

Gorgeous I was not. Huge, yes. Comforting to a woman in the same way they found a big guard dog reassuring. But gorgeous was never used without a hint of irony.

But that was Benta, and it was very much part of her charm.

She nodded toward the coffeemaker. "I started a pot so you'd have a warm mug when you go out to sun yourself."

She'd walk around my house naked but wouldn't touch me again until I was warm.

"Thank you," I said.

She checked each cabinet until she found my mugs. "You seem glum this morning," she said.

"Dog's still missing," I said.

"I'll go out with you. We'll track him," Benta said.

Her help would make finding him a lot easier. "Thank you," I said again.

She walked over and raised her hand as if to touch my arm, but pulled back her fingers. "If you need to talk about what happened to you with the pike, or this whole thing about your father building a vampire brother, I'm here."

I would have touched her face and kissed her lips, but Benta didn't like cold me. "Thank you." I seemed to be thanking her a lot.

"I'll get you that coffee."

I walked toward the kitchen doors. The bright sun shone down on a new day. We were close enough to September that the mornings had turned brisk, but the fresh air smelled of the lake and crisp leaves.

I threw open both doors and walked out onto the deck.

Marcus Aurelius bounded down the trail and up the steps.

"Hey, boy!" My dog came home.

He barked once and turned in a circle, then ran back down the trail. "Where are you going?" I was in my underwear and couldn't follow. "Come back here!"

A woman rounded the tree and stopped when she saw me standing on my deck.

The look on her face was remarkably similar to Benta's when she wanted physical contact, but this woman's face held a lot more than simple horniness.

I saw amazement, and happiness, and something I never thought I would ever see—appreciation. And for a second, I wondered what "gorgeous" meant to her.

"Frank," she said. "You're okay!" She ran up the deck and dropped her backpack as she moved toward me.

My backpack. I recognized the stain on the pocket.

"I saw the elves pull the pipe out of your chest before the pull finally took me but I didn't know for sure. I was so worried."

This woman who had run up onto my deck wrapped her arms around my chest and hugged me tightly.

She didn't pull away. She was shocked by my cold skin—I could tell—but she didn't let go. "The emperor spent the night with me. We were both worried," she said. "Right, boy?"

He barked.

"Who are you?" I didn't know this woman but I wanted to. I wanted to pick her up and spend the day like this, touching and talking, and making some sense of the world.

She stepped back. "Ellie Jones. The concealment enchantments wipe your memory every night." She smiled and touched my chest. "I'm your—"

She stopped talking when the still mostly-naked Benta walked out onto the deck.

"You forgot your coffee," Benta said. She walked down the deck and handed me the mug as if the woman who'd hugged me wasn't even there.

"Ah...." I said. Nothing came out. I couldn't point out that there was another person here, either.

The woman who called herself Ellie Jones stepped back. She pointed at Benta. "The enchantments always conceal me from magicals."

This time, Benta did touch my chest before bending over to pet my dog. "I thought I heard you barking." She scratched his ears. "You came home."

Ellie Jones picked up the backpack. She looked at me, then at my dog, then at Benta. Then she pulled my phone out of her pocket and set it on the deck rail. "I'm sorry," she said, and ran down the trail.

Benta nodded toward my mat in the patch of sun down by the lake. "Aren't you going to warm up?" she asked.

I watched Ellie Jones run away.

I was alive. I had a beautiful elf in my home. I'd survived the vampires. But something told me that what had just happened was worse than Dracula. Worse than the low-demons. Worse than anything.

And I had no idea what to do.

EPILOGUE

High noon, the day of Alfheim's magical reset...

The bright power of a magical cleansing hummed through the
air like the sound high-voltage powerlines made—that tingling,
wavering, upsetting buzz that only happens in a charged atmosphere.

Such times were the best for taking a stroll through the neighborhood.

No one bothered him most days, mostly because the other elder
elves preferred it that way. He was to be left alone, not talked to, not
to be encouraged to share his thoughts or ideas. And one was never to
ask him for help, or to fall for his tricks, or to invite him in, no matter
how entertaining he might be at a party.

He prided himself on his charm and hospitality, and on his ability
to dance well and to sing. His jokes were the best among the elves',
and his pranks legendary. And other elves had long found his black eyes
and gray hair to be, by themselves, a fascination they could not ignore.

So these spells his father worked so that no one bothered him
caused his heart to ache. But the spells were there for a reason—a
reason he was fully aware of and, in all honesty, supported.

Either he was not to be bothered, or they would have to kill him, and the elves, like the gods, did not kill their own. No, no, you did not kill your own. Lucky for him, some taboos were never meant to be broken.

His father had a big heart anyway, and felt his fatherly place among the elves was to be their leader. He was the bringer of civilization, and the elf who walked among the mundane. He lived with knowledge and memory, and would never turn away an elf or creature he felt might someday help him against the coming End Times.

Such was his father.

But in these times of resettings, the controls on "not bothering" relaxed. In these times, strolling the neighborhood became a viable option for the lonely.

He'd never been in this particular house, even though it had stood on this lake for two hundred years. It smelled of fae magic, and witch magic, and the unseemly practice of mixing. Not that he cared. Mixing was always entertaining, and the mixed man who lived here seemed to be a good person, a jotunn who, like him, had walked his trials and survived.

The house was lovely, if small. The table sat next to the wide doors and offered an also-lovely view of the lake.

Perhaps he and the owner could be friends.

He first touched the witch's notebook. She'd been a beacon for him, and one of the few in Alfheim who did not seem constrained by his father's call to "not bother" him. She'd been a beautiful woman, and strong, and it had pained him that he was not able to help her, in the end. He'd tried, early on. Offered what he could, and she'd told him she was proud to have been the one who found the good in his soul.

He had good in his soul. He had bad, too. At least he was man enough to admit it.

The other book, though, that one caught his attention. "Rygnyrök" scrolled across its leather cover in classic jotunn script, and he wondered if their town giant had a twinge in his stomach when he saw it. If, perhaps, the owner of this cabin was in fact what the joke said he was.

He picked up the book and tucked it under his arm. He needed new reading material, now that the library was closed and the younger brother of Lord Dracula was no longer around to suggest bodice rippers.

He was going to miss the vampires. They were almost as entertaining as he was. Well, Radu the Handsome had been entertaining, but not the fae-witch-born one. He'd been creepy and not an easy creature to read. Those who were not easy to read were the ones who hampered his pranks.

This new book would, though, give him hours and hours of enjoyment. Of this he was certain.

He touched the table and swirled up the threads of fae concealment enchantments hanging around this place.

No one would remember the book, now. Not his semi-sister, the other half-fae, and certainly not the jotunn, Frank Victorsson.

No, no one would know that Hrokr Arnesson had stopped by for a cup of sugar and a chat. No one at all.

He sighed as he looked out over this land's lovely lake. Sometimes, he missed the old country. There, they let him walk amongst the people.

He was the real reason his father did not return with his mundanes. He was the reason they came so deep into this New World. Either they fled, or his father stepped aside and allowed him to take his true name, his god name, his aspect: Hrokr Lokisson.

Maybe, yet, it would happen.

He patted his new book-friend and sniffed the tingly air. Time to return to his place of not-bothering and be ever-so-thankful that the elves thought like gods.

Because he was bored. And when Loki got bored, the world became very entertaining indeed.

~

Word of mouth and reviews are vital to the success of any author. If you enjoyed **Vampire Cursed** please consider leaving a review. Even one sentence would be useful for other readers.
Thank you!

JOIN FRANK VICTORSSON and the rest of Alfheim in **Elf Raised**....

ELF RAISED

Arne Odinsson's got some explainin' to do.

When the Kings call an international Conclave of Magicals, Arne and his people have no choice but to attend. Someone needs to explain why wolves, vampires, and witches have been allowed to live —and cause problems—in Alfheim.

Frank and Remy join Arne, Magnus, and a handful of Alfheim's other elves as they navigate not only elven politics, but also the kami, their new contacts from New Zealand, and a horde worse than vampires—cosplayers.

Because where would an international convention of magicals happen? At the world's largest international cosplay gathering, of course.

Welcome to Las Vegas's own "Elfcon," baby. May we all survive.

Elf Raised, available now…

GET FREE BOOKS

SUBSCRIBE TO KRIS AUSTEN RADCLIFFE'S NEWSLETTER

You will be notified when Kris Austen Radcliffe's next novel is released, as well as gain access to an occasional free bit of author-produced goodness. Your email address will never be shared and you can unsubscribe at any time.

WWW.SIXTALONSIGN.COM/MAILING-LIST-SIGN-UP/

THE WORLDS OF
KRIS AUSTEN RADCLIFFE

Smart Urban Fantasy:

Northern Creatures

Monster Born

Vampire Cursed

Elf Raised

Wolf Hunted

Fae Touched

Death Kissed

God Forsaken

Magic Scorned

Witch Burned (*coming soon*)

Genre-bending Science Fiction about
love, family, and dragons:

WORLD ON FIRE

Series one

Fate Fire Shifter Dragon

Games of Fate

Flux of Skin

Fifth of Blood

Bonds Broken & Silent

All But Human

Men and Beasts

The Burning World

Dragon's Fate and Other Stories

Series Two

Witch of the Midnight Blade

Witch of the Midnight Blade Part One

Witch of the Midnight Blade Part Two

Witch of the Midnight Blade Part Three

Witch of the Midnight Blade: The Complete Series

Series Three

World on Fire

Call of the Dragonslayer (*coming soon*)

Hot Contemporary Romance:

The Quidell Brothers

Thomas's Muse

Daniel's Fire

Robert's Soul

Thomas's Need

Quidell Brothers Box Set

Includes:

Thomas's Muse

Daniel's Fire

Roberts's Soul

ABOUT THE AUTHOR

Kris's Science Fiction universe, **World on Fire**, brings her descriptive touch to the fantastic. Her Urban Fantasy series, **Northern Creatures**, sets her magic free. She's traversed many storytelling worlds including dabbles in film and comic books, spent time as a talent agent and a textbook photo coordinator, as well written nonfiction. But she craved narrative and richly-textured worlds—and unexpected, true love.

Kris lives in Minnesota with one husband, two daughters, and three cats.

For more information
www.krisaustenradcliffe.com